Layers of Darkness

Roger Johnson

ISBN 978-1-7364368-8-2 (paperback)

email: rogerj47@gmail.com
website: Roger_Johnson.com

To the Parents and Families . . .

ACKNOWLEDGMENTS

My continued appreciation to my small group of readers who offer their insightful critiques and heartfelt encouragement.

Special thanks to my formatter Joe DesGeorges.
Cover design by the Artist Always Known as Joe DesGeorges

Books by Roger Johnson

Laments for the Dead

The Cheetah Basketball Series
On Point
Gifts
Coach Izzy

Other Books in the Queue include
America's Soul
Jegos
The Hill, '67
Lines
Seeds and Hoops (working title)

Layers of Darkness

Roger Johnson

IngramSpark

2022

Layers of Darkness

"Still, I wonder about the Darkness, about where it
came from."

Hogan Tree

Chapter 1

The smaller man scrambles on all fours to elude the enraged animal who has already broken his nose and cut his bicep with the jagged beer bottle. Patrons of The Jungle move away to the walls for protection; they want no part of the rage, just as most of the people of the town want no part of The Jungle. The bleeding man, a Vietnam veteran new in town, didn't anticipate his opponent's craziness. Sitting at the bar sharing beers and stories about their war when no one else seemed interested, reminiscing about fire fights and Zippo raids, flipped the insane switch on Fulton Tree. He perceived the comments as insults, defended the indiscriminate violence of Nam, and surprised the man with a backhand across this face, knocking him off his stool.

Fulton tosses a table aside to get at the defenseless man whose terrified eyes plead for an end. Fulton kicks him twice, then bends down and slugs him hard to the side of his face, and a cheek bone cracks loudly. Three men break from the wall to tackle Fulton, hoping to end the carnage, only to be batted away like so many flies. As the animal turns back to the man who lays curled on the floor in the fetal position, he is clubbed over the head by the stock end of a shotgun. Fulton falls to the floor unconscious. "Haven't you had enough blood for one day, you dumbass?"

It's an hour past midnight on this tragic day in Eagle Canyon, Colorado, in the summer of 1977.

§

Random Tree's little head lies against his mother's breast, his red, curly hair still matted with traces of blood. His body jerks sporadically, too frequently for a normal boy of eight. Small for his age, Burelle Oakley cuddles him tightly, her cheek on his head. She has him now, but she knows he is not completely safe, and with good reason. In the rocking chair, their two hearts beat as one, keeping time with the rockers as they move slowly and regularly on the wood floor in the dim light. What is it about a rocking chair that unites a mother and child so intimately, as if no others exist?

They aren't alone tonight, however. Police Officer Esch sits a room away at the kitchen table with her back to the wall. She sips coffee and makes notes in a small pocket pad. She keeps a straight-line view of Burelle and Random, the gentlest of the Trees, as today proved. The range light casts a gray pallor over the kitchen, an ashen complement to the darker living room. Mother and son will be the talk of the town for the weeks and months ahead. The towns-people will gather to gossip, to tell each other how this happened. Small town surety, but they won't really know. These are not good economic times in Eagle Canyon. The last local mine closed in the spring. It scares people into believing crazy and blaming others. They want clear and simple answers; they want a quick solution, but for today's event, there won't be any.

The officer rises to stretch and refill her coffee. She sets it down on the table and walks into the parlor to reassure Burelle and Random. Standing behind the rocker, Esch gently puts her hand on Burelle's shoulder. Burelle tilts her head slightly to acknowledge the touch. The two women have a history, years of friendship, but more. Only Esch's head and neck rise above Burelle's head. If they were standing side-by-side, Burelle would tower over Esch. Random's eyes open with his mother's movement. He takes note of Esch, readjusts his body against his mother's bosom, and falls back asleep. Esch stays momentarily, squeezes Burelle's shoulder, and then returns to her protective position at the kitchen table.

A father should be here instead of me, thinks Esch, but that would require that he gives a damn about his son. It's better for Burelle and Random anyway, since Fulton would just turn the blame somehow to Burelle and yell. News like this travels fast, and even a drunk will hear. Better tonight that Fulton isn't here. Much better. She studies her friend, whose eyes are wide open and whose jaw is steeled. God! Life isn't fair, and it certainly hasn't been for Burelle. Esch tries to be professional for this, but she and Burelle were once best friends. Burelle's pregnancy and her move into the big house put distance between them. Mostly that move to the big house owned by the Trees.

Burelle won't sleep. Like a fox whose kit has been severely threatened, she remains alert. Her dark eyes see images in the night, images of the past, figures of danger. She understands why Esch stays nearby, but Burelle wonders if Esch could protect Random. Protecting Random. That's Burelle's mission. He was born tiny and remains small for his age. Burelle sees threats, where her son does not. He sees life. About his dad, Random is vigilant, but not for his own safety. For his mom's. Maybe he protects her as she protects him. But she has been hurt, while he hasn't. She knows life has its dangers; she knows that so well. The traditions and unspoken policies of a small town prevent outside forces from intervening, and Eagle Canyon is definitely a small town. The past and the present have merged, as they always do, and Burelle no longer wants to accept violence as her way of life. She has lived with it so long, all her life, and she feels utterly and absolutely alone.

Burelle thinks of the other mothers, four others whose children either died or were injured. Random emerged the least harmed, and for this she is eternally grateful. She doesn't know any of the other mothers personally. Now, she thinks, we are a club, but one that no one else wants to join. Who comforts those mothers? Who hugs them? Since reuniting with Random, no one has hugged her. No one except her child.

§

The little boy's eyes remain wide open; they gather in every aspect of the violence. He blinks with each explosion. His head flinches to the right or left when a body is hit and torn apart. He doesn't understand, but he absorbs each detail. He keeps his hands on his Sunday school teacher's back. To his left hide two friends, each trying to be invisible to the shooter, both crying as they are all pushed against the wall. A shot tears away the teacher's shoulder, splattering blood on the three boys. She falls back against them. The little boy unwedges himself just as another round strikes his teacher's neck, passing through and splintering the wooden wall. He scoots to her side, lifts her head, and rests it on his lap. He looks up at the shooter, silently asking him why.

The shooter raises his rifle again, but then looks over it. He wears a blue bandana around his face so only his eyes are visible between the handkerchief and the rifle barrel. Those eyes accidently catch the eyes of the boy. "You shouldn't be here," he whispers.

"No," says the little boy. "You shouldn't be here. Go home."

"I can't." He lowers his weapon. "Where's Pastor Chamberlain?" he asks as if the boy should know. The shooter pivots away and asks the question again, but this time he screams to the entire room. He turns to the door, steps over the lifeless body of an older boy, and leaves.

Commotion ensues in the hall, but in the room the little boy does not seem to hear it. He wipes some blood and flesh from the face of his teacher and then pushes her eyelids shut.

§

Russo races up Interstate-70 west of Eagle Canyon in complete disregard for the fifty-five mile-per-hour speed limit. He has his three-year-old cruiser back, the '74 Plymouth Fury, 360 V-8, with the whole package. His cruiser, his highway, his time—Sunday mornings, the only day of the week he doesn't work. His car was sideswiped by a sixteen-year-old who was taking her driver's exam nearly two weeks earlier, but it's healthy again. This Sunday, while his town goes to church, Russo forgoes the gospels and drives.

"Shots fired, Chief. Possible casualties!" Panic alters the dispatcher's voice. Seventeen years on the force and Police Chief Russo has never received a call like this. Eighteen years earlier he covered a shooting that left three teenage boys dead, all shot with junk guns in a poor neighborhood where violence was common, even accepted. Summer violence, nightly incidents. But that was Chicago. Few people outside of those neighborhoods cared.

Seven minutes after receiving the call, the beefy, balding police chief kneels over the body of Bradley Arnold, a good friend's son, who lies in a pool of blood. The boy is barely recognizable from his wounds, but Russo brushes Bradley's matted hair up onto his head, leaves his hand there, and says a quick prayer. Russo hears the question screamed from a porch in that Chicago neighborhood from a distraught woman eighteen years ago. "What you gonna do about this, Officer? What you gonna do about my children?"

CHAPTER 2

On the day before the shooting, like he does on most summer weekends, Hogan Tree walks to the river with his dog, Tinker, in silence. Despite a painful hip and a slight limp, which makes it seem like he's carrying an uneven weight, Hogan moves purposely, as if there is a destination. He is a quiet man, and the townspeople of Eagle Canyon respect his privacy. He is the custodian for Whitman Elementary School; he has been for as long as most can remember. Hogan frequently works nights or helps out at the high school. A rumor began years earlier that Hogan keeps a cot in the boiler room at school. His neighbors hadn't observed him returning home from work at nights. Whitman Elementary is spotless and efficient, and those who work there know who is responsible for this. Small towns take pride in their schools; they are the gathering places for nearly every special event, from political meetings to their kids' plays and games. Eagle Canyon is such a town. It got its name from the stately birds that once controlled the canyon, before the miners altered the landscape and forced them away. Hogan hasn't seen an eagle soaring above the river since he was a teenager nearly forty years ago.

Twenty-Six Mile Creek runs through the middle of Eagle Canyon, entering from the west and exiting to the east, toward Denver. It is a misnamed river, short-changed by some forty miles as it flows from the continental divide, down the steep-walled canyons, through Golden and into Denver where it quietly joins the South Platte River on its long journey to the Missouri-Mississippi and the Gulf of Mexico. It constantly reminds Hogan that people and things are a part of something much larger than themselves. He enjoys the seasons of the river, the heavy flows in late spring-early summer when the snow melt carves the land, cuts the banks, and grinds up the rocks, which eventually get carried away over time, away from Eagle Canyon to be replaced by rocks from higher in the canyon. After the runoff Twenty-Six Mile Creek eases, and it becomes a fisherman's creek with small trout. On occasion Hogan wades the creek hoping to hook one of these fish. Poisoned from decades of mining in the area, it never became a great fishery, but it has rejuvenated itself over time, and Denver people come to enjoy its waters in the canyons. Hogan always selects a stone early in his walk to carry in his pocket, a pebble worn smooth by the action of erosion. At the end of his walk, he will remove the stone and toss it into the middle of the river for good luck, a habit given to him by his wife years ago. A cement bike/jogging path was constructed in the early seventies, but Hogan seldom uses it. At the river he pauses to stare into the waters and contemplate, and to throw a stick for Tinker to retrieve. Tourists who bike the path often wave at Hogan, and he will raise his hand in return. Hogan is not unfriendly, simply a solitary person. He has his own spot, about a half-mile down from town where the river bends around a hill, dipping well below the bike path to hide from the interstate. In a white plastic lawn chair that he put there years earlier, he sits to read or write his weekly letter to Gertie, his wife. Despite the August heat, it is cool and relaxing by the river, but on this day his insides churn. He has a premonition, a feeling that things could spin out of control soon.

Earlier in the day, Hogan's son created a public commotion at the grocery store. Fulton Tree lives to create problems; he thrives on his reputation as a tough guy. Fulton doesn't live with Hogan. He lives with his grandfather, Morvid Tree, in the big house on the hill, one of Eagle Canyon's most stately manors. Also living in the big house are Fulton's eight-year-old son, Random Tree, and Random's mother, Burelle Oakley. It was Burelle whom Fulton berated in the produce department over her choice of foods that she was feeding Random. Burelle brought Random to Hogan's house for a respite. Hogan's small house is four blocks from Morvid's and nearer to downtown. Random often visits there, where he and his grandpa read books or play catch inside the picket fence—while Burelle breathes.

Fulton never enters his father's house; he knows better, so Burelle and Random have one safe place to go. Today, they stayed until the afternoon and had lunch before returning to Morvid's house. When they left, Hogan went for his customary walk. He carries a satchel over his shoulder which contains his book of the week and a note-pad. When he arrives at his river spot, Hogan pulls out his pad and begins to write furiously, another letter, not to his wife, but to the West Denver Institute, a hospital he's written to before, and a place he knows well. He is much too agitated to write to Gertie yet. "I have contacted you before and talked with three doctors from the Institute, but I get nowhere. My son has struggled with anger and detachment his whole life . . ."

Hogan's river place contains an established stand of aspen and a smaller one of narrow-leaf cottonwoods. He selected his spot years earlier in part because of these trees; the aspen have grown and spread substantially in the decade-plus that he has come to this spot. Their gray-whitish trunks contain black "eyes" that seem to be watching him, or as he often tells Random, "watching out for him." The river carves out a larger bend each year imperiling the roots of Hogan's stand, and when these roots are fully exposed, his aspen will die. Still, he figures he'll outlive the process of nature in his little world, and his aspen forest will survive long after he has passed and probably long after Random has moved on. Random once asked how long that would be. "Randy, my boy, it's hard to say. Time is illusory. It's a gauge, a benchmark Time is what has already occurred, not what lies ahead. You will live your life out the way God intends, and each day will be a time. We take advantage of today, our time in the world, and go forward" Random was too young to understand, and it showed on his face. Hogan tousled his grandson's red hair, smiled, and said, "This river will flow all the way to the ocean. That is its time. You will live until you get to Heaven, and that will be your time."

The cottonwoods and aspen seem similar in many ways, like the people of Eagle Canyon, but they originate from different places, from different roots, and they grow with their own distinctive styles. Hogan read about these trees, considered their rapid growth, but relatively short lives, and he began to appreciate them beyond their colors. Earlier in the summer, he wrote Gertie to express some concern about his aspen grove, that some of the leaves had a brown tint to them. She replied that aspen propagate through their roots, and once a tree is diseased, it can infect the entire grove. Gertie told him to ignore it, that it was more than likely a simpler reason, like insects.

He finishes his letter to the Institute, seals it, and tucks it into his satchel. He takes Gertie's last letter out and rereads it. As always, she worries about him in America, a place she often compares to New Zealand's native people, the Maori, and to New Zealand's larger sibling, Australia: beautiful, but flawed with all its angry men. These men protect their right to defend any perceived slight through violence. Her father and grandfather and the men of the region were soldiers, but when they finished their service, they came home to the ranch and were hardworking and honorable. Gertie was distressed about her time away from her family and didn't thrive living it in Eagle Canyon. Hogan understood it then, and he is stressed about recent behaviors today. She closes as she usually does, with her love and plea for him to hurry back to her, to be by her side again.

Hogan takes up his pen and writes, "Plans are underway. I need to take care of Fulton before I return to your arms. I have to break this chain."

CHAPTER 3

Inside the police station where they were rushed for protection when the shots rang out, congregants huddle in families just as they had minutes earlier in the church. Quiet prayers are being said as they beseech the Lord to intervene to keep their children safe. Not Burelle though. She stands alone in the narrow hall that connects the main office with the cellblock. Like a servant at a formal state dinner. The practiced art of silence, of non-existence. Pushed to the back of the room, this is where she waits for Random and watches these families. She knows this building well.

The hallway reminds her of the hall in her old, single-wide trailer, her home before Morvid's. Maybe her only home. Narrow like the walls that give Eagle Canyon its distinctive character, narrow like her life. Someone yells out, "Chief Russo just drove up to the church!" as if everything will be all right now. Burelle wants to push forward to see but does not. She knows things are not all right and won't get any better because the chief of police magically appeared. The damage is done, just as it was so many years before when she was in this hallway, sent here by Chief Russo, so that he could speak with her parents in private. Oh, Random, she fears. Oh, Burelle, she remembers.

My life to here has been so messy, but it wasn't entirely my fault. Am I talking to God, she wonders? If not God, then who? Fulton called me a slut, but I wasn't. I was a teenager who matured early and wanted to be touched, even if it was inappropriately. I liked to be felt up, but I wasn't a slut. Just needy. Just like all the average-looking junior high girls from poor homes whose parents have divorced. Scared.

There aren't any young children in the room. A few babies, a few teenagers, but the children Random's age were in the Bible studies classes during communion. "Suffer little children," she recalls; something about Heaven belonging to them. "No!" she screams.

Heads turn to Burelle. A middle-aged lady walks to her, puts an arm around Burelle's shoulders, and ushers her to the window where the lady's husband stands. Burelle recognizes them from church but does not know their names. Do they have children in the church wing? "It will be okay," says the husband to comfort Burelle. The immediate evidence does not support his optimism: police activity, an ambulance, separation.

Burelle's mother was the eternal optimist in the face of overwhelming evidence to the contrary. "It will be all right, honey." But it never was. Burelle's father was an abusive drunk, violence mostly perpetrated against her mother, but not always. Burelle would watch them fight, a big woman always losing to a smaller, angry man. The outcome was never in doubt, but Burelle's mother waged the war each time like she enjoyed something about the battle. When her father went after her, though, Burelle's mother never stepped in. She didn't protect me, remembers Burelle, or at least I don't remember it if she did.

All these people, thinks Burelle, all these mothers. Any secrets? It doesn't seem so in church. Just mine. The bad girl. Daddy told me. Fulton tells Random. "You're a sissy. How can you be my boy?" Not really a question, but an accusation.

The husband yells, "Someone's coming out! He's carrying a child!"

It's Hogan. It's Random. And he's covered in blood. Burelle remembers her science teacher from her sophomore year, Mr. Switzer, the man who truly worried for Burelle after she got pregnant. Mr. Switzer is holding up bloody hands in the lab and smiling. "Now, I will remove its heart."

Burelle faints.

§

It's a fog now. Who is the boy that is being pushed toward the police station? Where is Hogan taking me and Random? Is this a dance? It seems like I'm floating.

§

"Watch your step, Burelle. Move, Tinker. Sit here at the table while I clean up Random a bit. He's not hurt, Burelle. Put your head down if you get dizzy again. I'll just be right here at the kitchen sink."

§

The fog lifts. Burrelle stands and walks unsteadily to Random and Hogan. She slides her hands into the running tap water and then rubs them over her son's arms and face to help remove the blood. Hogan has taken off Random's church clothes, and they lie on the floor next to the refrigerator. Random looks into his mother's face, maybe searching for an answer. Instead, he finds some strength there. Burelle stops her hands on Random's cheeks and then bends to put her forehead on Random's forehead. "You had me worried, sweetheart." Her voice is barely audible even to Hogan who stands at her shoulder still washing his grandson.

"It was really scary, Mom." His eyes see the event again. "Grampa came and got me."

"We were all scared, but you're safe now. Grampa brought you to me."

"I'm going to get a towel. Then, I'll put his clothes in the laundry. No sense for you to go back to Morvid's today. We'll stay here away from all the commotion." Hogan dries his hands on a dishrag and leaves the kitchen.

"Are you okay?" asks Random.

§

For every violent act that has occurred in Burelle's life, she has known the perpetrator. But not today, and it confuses her. She doesn't know the proper response. It feels like she has lost something. She hugs her son more tightly to her body and waits for Hogan to return with a new set of clothes Not once has she thought about Fulton or Morvid; only about her own mother and father and the lifeline that flows through her body into her son's.

CHAPTER 4

Earlier in the summer, a university senior-to-be sits down with Morvid Tree, Hogan's father, Fulton's grandfather, and Random's great-grandfather, to hear and record the saga of one family from Eastern Europe that has made a successful life in America. The journalism student will earn credit for independent study over the summer; how hard can it be to listen to an eighty-year-old man ramble on about his life in America? The student has a notebook with written questions, but the old man needs no prompts. The student raises his palms for a quick delay, switches on his portable recorder, nods his head for Mr. Tree to begin, and leans back to enjoy the story. He wonders how much the old man will accurately be able to remember. Morvid gives the student a hand-made drawing, a diagram of the family tree, titled, "The American Tree," and clears his throat.

"My name is Morvid Tree. I'm a tired, old man wearing out of that very age. I will tell you of the Tree's journey from the Old Country to America and of our lives here in this great country. The history of the Trees is what I say it is. I'm the vault, the record keeper, the truth. I am the Trees' trunk, and everyone is a branch of me." Tree wears a narrow-lapelled, dark blue suit with a bolo tie and black suspenders. Strands of gray hair are combed straight back and slicked down. He sports a Walt Disney-like mustache, and his blue eyes narrow as if he's about to reveal a secret. He believes his story is important; that his family's history is important. "As a boy I was drafted to fight in France—in The Great War. Over there, in the trenches, I learned to dance, but I'm getting ahead of myself. I should start with the cabin."

§

After lunch Morvid waits with his coffee while the student adjusts his recorder and lays out his notebook again. The student sips a convenience store soda, politely refusing Morvid's coffee offer, and sits down at the old man's kitchen table. Despite the summer afternoon heat, the house remains remarkably cool. The morning session went well, and now the old man is eager to continue. While Mr. Tree speaks, the student studies his subject. Heavily wrinkled, liver spots, bloodshot eyes, slightly stooped at the shoulders. There is more to Morvid's story than will be revealed in his words.

"Our Polish name was unpronounceable, so Pap shortened it to Tree when he and my ma and me got off the boat in Baltimore in ninety-nine. He swore he wasn't Polish, that he was German, but it didn't really matter; the people in western Massachusetts called all of us Polacks. I should say them because I was too young to remember. Your professor wants the background, so here it is in a nutshell. Ma and Pap were Catholic, but they seldom practiced. His people were poor in the Old Country. He moved to the city as a young boy to work in the factories, since the family didn't own land. He ended up working in a mine somewhere up in Prussia. Pap never learned to read or write well, so he just told me this when we were building the cabin. I looked it up, some of the stuff he told me that summer, but I never got to ask him again. Evidently, Pap and a brother left Europe to escape conscription; all the poor people in Europe got drafted, I guess, and he came to America for a new life. He wanted to escape the violence of Eastern Europe. He first settled in a town called Deerfield, but he never fit in, so he took us to Pennsylvania to work in the mines. That's where he learned to speak English, and it's what he did for the rest of his life; he was a miner. I was born in either '96 or '97, but my birth certificate doesn't exist, so I was always an American. When The Great War broke out in 1914, Pap feared that America would be drawn in eventually, so he moved us as far away from back east as he could, thinking he could hide me from war by being farther from the government. Anyway, that's how the family ended up in Colorado, here in Eagle Canyon. Pap got a job in the mine here.

"Pap was tall and wiry, maybe not as tall as me, but tall for the time. He would laugh and say that he was the first Tree planted in America, and he hoped his forest would grow thick here. I was the first born; I have four sisters who married and had large families and moved away, and one brother who died of the flu just after the war. He was the youngest. When Pap was killed, I became the patriarch, the man in charge, and that's what I've remained for the last fifty-eight years.

"Anyway, back to the cabin. Pap and I built it in the summer of 1917 out by the lake. President Wilson declared war on Germany in April, and Pap had a premonition, so he decided to make that summer a special one for the two of us. Pap talked of me returning to the Old Country and that he might never see me again. He quit his job at the mine, told Ma that she would have to work odd jobs to make ends meet, that he and I would live in a tent and build this cabin. It was the best summer of my life.

"Pap and I worked long days, sometimes up to sixteen hours. We loaded up his tools on a wagon and hooked up a mule and drove them out to the lake. He had made a deal with some fella in town to buy lumber that was mostly cured and that was already on the site. I don't remember the details, but we only had to haul it a short distance to our spot. Where he got the money for the wood, I can't say, since we were poor. Pap wanted it done before summer ended; he wanted to have it complete before the snows fell, so we didn't build a real foundation. We set the floor on big, wooden stumps and built up from there. During the day we sawed and planed the wood, erected the walls, built window frames and door jambs, and made a stone fireplace. In the evening we fished, drank and smoked, looked at the night sky, and I learned as much as I could about Pap's life in Europe. He was a great storyteller. Oh, one other thing. We wrestled, usually when we'd had too much to drink, and he always beat me pretty good. On the weekends we would ride home to see Ma and the girls. It was on one of those weekends when my brother was conceived.

"It was a beautiful cabin. Just one large room, but big enough for a kitchen table, a stove, and two large beds: one for Pap and Ma, and one for us children. Pap said that if I was uncomfortable with that, I could sleep outside in the tent. Because we built it so quickly, Pap said that it would be a work in progress; that we would have to make repairs each summer to complete it. We finished in August, the same month I got my draft notice, and we went to town to get Ma and the girls. We spent two days here in Eagle Canyon and then packed a food basket and headed back to the lake to spend our first night in the cabin.

"I sensed something was wrong before we got to the cabin. When we arrived, we found the cabin had been shot all to hell sometime in the last two days. Hundreds of bullet holes had ruined the frame. The windows were all shattered. The door had been pulled out to gain entrance. Inside, everything was torn up or turned over. Whoever had done it, and Pap found out later, had shit on the floor and poured the rest of the paint and varnish all over. You can't imagine how we felt. After just a few minutes, Pap ordered me to take Ma and the girls back home, that he would take care of it. Reluctantly, I did, leaving him behind to begin the cleanup. Sometime that evening, he burned the cabin to the ground. My guess is he sat and watched it burn all night.

"That September I married Danver Wylkes, a rich, older woman from lower Germany whose husband had died, and I inherited three children. I left for the Army shortly after."

§

Morvid returns to the kitchen table from the bathroom and asks the student where they left off. The student reminds him, clicks on his tape recorder, and the old man continues. Like Morvid, the student is first generation American and proud of his country, only his tree's roots are in Mexico. The student's family history will be recorded more accurately through journals, photos, videos, and modern technology. Even so, there will be gaps and misinterpretations.

"The Great War turned out to be my life's great adventure, but I sure wouldn't have believed that when I boarded the train in Denver, which took me to Kansas for my training. Ma had baked me some cookies for the trip, and Pap told me that he didn't reckon we would see each other ever again, but that he hoped we would. War back then destroyed families. After four months of training, the Army shipped us boys to New York where we were loaded onto a steamer that took us to France. Some captain slapped me on the back on the dock and said that if the ship was hit by torpedoes, swim like hell. I didn't think it was funny at all, since I'd never learned to swim.

"Seeing cities for the first time was incredible. Although I didn't get into the city, I just saw it from the train and the port, New York's tall buildings and hordes of people flabbergasted me. I had no recollection of cities from my early childhood. When we arrived off the coast of France, we couldn't disembark immediately, and I stayed on the ship for almost two weeks. In France after trains took us near to our camps, we marched through Paris to get to our camps south of there. I promised myself that if I survived, I would return to Paris as a civilian and walk every boulevard.

"We trained hard. General Pershing was this ghost on a horse that we all held in awe. We lived in tents, ate out of cans, and got dysentery. On our infrequent leaves, we were entertained by the YMCA girls who had come over on the boats to keep our spirits up, but there were so few of them and lots of French girls. Eventually, we went to the front during the summer of '18 and became heroes. I saw action in most of the American battles, but the worst was at St. Mihiel and the Meuse-Argonne. I kept seeing Pap and thinking I'd never see him again. You can read your history books to understand how terrible that fighting was. Us Americans were fresh and never had to undergo the years in the trenches. We experienced some of it, but mostly we were on the move. The old armies from both sides were worn out. I do remember watching the French soldiers and thinking how brave they were and how terribly they were led. I got to know a few, and some British soldiers too, but the Frenchies were special. Fighting on their land, in their own country, it was like there was a sickness that no one wanted to treat, a silent, unspoken sickness. Sunken eyes, thinning hair, old before their time. I think they knew their country was beaten and wouldn't recover quickly.

The killing was no longer achieving anything for them. Yeah, they might win the war, but they had lost their souls. Eastern France had become their hell.

"In the fall of '18, we began to hear rumors of an armistice. I think the Americans, because of our naivety and illusions of right and wrong in wartime, were optimistic. The French and British hoped for it but remained skeptical. There was never a war more awful than The Great War, and excuse me if I keep calling it The Great War instead of World War I like you learned, but that's what we called it until Hitler and the Nazis started the next one. The Frenchies didn't know what life they would be returning to. Hell, most of them were injured in some way, often in places you couldn't see, and so many of their brothers had been killed. By the time we arrived in France, their army was made up of old men and young teenagers. The core of their men, the men who should be fighting, was gone, used up in the first years of fighting.

"The armistice did come. I remember fighting right up to the end on pointless missions. 'Once more over the top,' 'one more flanking movement,' 'try to capture two hundred more yards of territory' that had been fought over for four years. Politicians killed more good men than the Germans. Anyway, the guns fell silent, and quickly we began to emerge from the bunkers and trenches, and we danced. Fiddles showed up magically. A French soldier grabbed me as he would a barroom prostitute and held me and spun me around to a tune. The whole line of soldiers danced. The Great War had ended, and a lot of us just wanted to go home. But not me; I wanted to go to Paris.

"Paris after the war was two cities. There was the terrible, crushing sadness for what was lost if you were French. Supposedly, France was on the winning side, but there was no victory for so many of them. Yeah, they had parades, but you could see it if you really looked. They were beaten just as surely as if they'd have been overrun by the German Huns, and their society wasn't going to recover any time soon. The other side of Paris was for me. The city hadn't been damaged much and the women were plentiful. I don't want to brag because any healthy male could have had as many conquests as I did, but the women of Paris opened their arms to me and many other American soldiers. That's not all they opened.

"I neglected to tell you that I was AWOL. I was young still, but I pretty much knew I was never going to make it back to Paris once I got back on that boat to America. A life of responsibility awaited me in Eagle Canyon, Colorado, in the U.S. of A., and I wanted to experience this complete freedom before I returned to that. After all, I'd earned it. I'd put my life on the line, and I believed that I deserved it. You need to look the other way with soldiers for what they do. Not just the killing on the battlefields, but for their actions with the locals. Soldiers need a little latitude. After a few weeks, I'd been taken in by a mademoiselle whose husband was killed near Verdun. His name was Jaures, and that's what she called me. She spoke almost no English, and I spoke even less French. She'd been lonely long enough. I stayed with her until the MPs found me and dragged me back to camp. I was busted a rank and given extra duty, but it had all been worth it. It was then that I received the letter from my Ma that Pap had been murdered."

CHAPTER 5

From the darkness of Hogan's living room, Burelle calls out softly. "Escher." Still in her blood-stained, law enforcement uniform, Esch comes and places a hard-backed chair opposite Burelle. "I haven't had much of a chance to say thanks," whispers Burelle. "It must have been the most awful thing for you." Hogan's small house serves as a refuge for Burelle and Random at times when they feel threatened.

Esch blinks hard and nods. "Yeah, it was. Both the acolytes are dead, and you know Mrs. Tuttle died. Pastor Chamberlain hid when he heard the gunfire, so the boy couldn't find him. I guess he was the main target."

"How are the two other boys?" asks Burelle.

"Injured, but it doesn't look like either is serious. Marty appears to have been shot in the arm, and that was pretty bad, but Kevin's wound looked worse than it actually was. He may not have been shot after all, just splinters from a ricochet maybe. There was just so much blood that it was hard to tell at the time. God, Burelle, there were pieces of flesh spattered on the walls."

"Random hasn't spoken about it, and I haven't asked. I thought I'd let it come out slowly." Burelle hasn't cried, but tears form in her eyes a couple of times. "Mrs. Tuttle saved him, didn't she?"

"It's hard to say, but it appears as if she tried to shield him and the two other boys with her body. They were grouped together in the corner, away from the older boys. Chief Russo said that the shooter mumbled something about the older boys being in robes and some people deserved what they got, but he doesn't know. We don't really know anything." Esch breathes hard again and brings her hands to her mouth as if to wipe something from her chin. "It's not rational, Burelle, but I keep blaming Pastor Chamberlain for hiding, for not doing something to save those acolytes." Hogan's dog appears and lies down next to the rocking chair. Esch reaches over and pets Tinker's ears. "I know that's not fair to Pastor, but it's how I feel. It was his house, and he hid."

Burelle puts her chin to Random's head. "He's finally sleeping soundly. He's stopped shaking and jerking. Do we know anything about the shooter?"

"It was Robbie Hollins. He's from here and things will come out. I just can't say much yet. I knew him once, but I don't think you did. He's in his late teens, a little younger than us. You'd recognize him maybe." Esch pauses as if she is rewinding the scene from the morning, from a half a day earlier. Burelle waits. "Some people said he was in church earlier. We don't know that. We have his name, and we're doing all the checking."

"Why? Why in Eagle Canyon? This isn't the place for that? And in church. Did he say?"

Esch shakes her head. "No, Burelle. He didn't say. After he shot up the room where Random was, it appears that he left to find Pastor Chamberlain, at least that's what we think. Kevin said he started yelling after he stopped shooting; kept demanding to know where Pastor Chamberlain was. When he left the Sunday school room and went out into the hallway, he bumped into the two men who were running to see what was happening, and they subdued him. They saved some lives, we're pretty sure of that."

"How old are the two boys?" Burelle can't bring herself to say, "who died," but Esch understands.

"Both were junior high students. You know their families. The shooter shot them both and then re-shot them to make sure they were dead. It's all so sick." Esch chokes up. Burelle extends her left hand to her friend, and Esch slides out of her chair and kneels in front of Burelle, placing her head on Burelle's knee. The officer cries for the first time and her body heaves. Burelle places her hand on the officer's head and strokes her hair, giving Esch time. It has been years since Burelle witnessed Esch cry.

Time, thinks Burelle. Many years earlier, this scene was reversed. After that night in the woods, I needed Esch, and it was Esch who held me all night. It was Esch who promised to take care of me. I knew she couldn't, but I wanted to believe it that night. We pretended that night, and then woke up the next morning hoping it hadn't happened. We learned to say motherfucker that morning and used it at every opportunity. It made us laugh and act tough, as if we could handle our problems. We had a secret, strengthened by a blood oath, never to tell. We pricked our fingers and held them together and thereafter called it "camping" when it needed to be discussed. Once again, Burelle feels the rage that often takes over her body, a rage she can never control or adequately respond to.

Finally, Esch's crying eases and her breathing slows. Without looking up at Burelle, she begins to tell her story. "Sorry, I guess fatigue sort of overwhelmed me. When I got to the church this morning, I had to get through the people in the room so we could investigate. Chief Russo arrested Robbie, and I went into the room. You think people get shot, and it's like on television, but it's not. It was so messy; the two boys who died were hardly recognizable. Burelle, he shot them in their faces. The people who were in the room were wailing and someone had thrown up. Every victim had someone holding them. Random was sitting in the corner holding Mrs. Tuttle's head in his lap. He was talking to her, but she was already dead. He was covered with blood, and I thought he had been shot. Mrs. Roth was trying to soothe him. I went to him first, and he said he was okay. That's what he said, Burelle, 'I'm okay.' He was so brave. Then I checked on Kevin and Marty, and I knew they were alive. The emergency personnel showed up right after that and began working on them. That's when Hogan grabbed my arms and turned me around. He spoke, Burelle, he spoke. He said, 'It will be all right,' and I calmed down and did my work. He bent down and lifted Random and took him out of the room. I didn't see Random again until I came over here." Esch eases back into a crouch and looks up at Burelle. "He brought Random to you, didn't he? Where is Hogan now?"

"He's sitting on the back porch. When he heard you arrive, he told me he'd stay out there," says Burelle. "I was just inside the church when we heard the shots, waiting to greet Pastor Chamberlain after the service. When we heard the shots, I panicked. I knew Random was there, but the men pushed us out the door toward the police station. I couldn't go back, so I waited in the station with the others. I don't know how Hogan got to Random, but he showed up at the station with him and brought us here." Burelle's eyes are glazed as if she exists in another place. Sharing her thoughts and feelings is not a part of her nature, even with her closest friend. Esch leans forward again and places her hands on Burelle's thighs. Burelle speaks again. "Do you know how hard it is not knowing whether your child is alive, to know you can't be there to protect him?"

Esch reaches up to touch Burelle's lips, to tell her to hush. Burelle allows Esch's fingers to remain on her lips, but those lips quiver, and tears drip from her eyes. She sees again Hogan hurrying toward the police station carrying Random; sees again her boy covered in blood. "I didn't leave the station to go to him, Esch. I thought . . ."

"Shhhh, now, Burelle. Random is okay. He's with you. Shhhh."

§

Whitman Elementary sits across the street from the Lutheran church, and Hogan is working on Sunday morning, catching up on those little tasks that don't seem to get done during the work week. He carries two plastic trash sacks out the back gym door to the dumpster. Across the street he sees Reverend Chamberlain scurrying around the church to get to the front of the church to greet his flock after the service. Hogan has never been inside the Lutheran church, but he knows his grandson will be finishing up his Bible lessons in one of the outer rooms. He lifts the heavy metal lid and throws in the sacks. Someone has left personal trash next to the container, so he bends down and lifts these grocery sacks into the dumpster. Some of the trash has spilled out onto the asphalt, and he picks this litter up. Earlier that morning he watched a hawk devour a small bird on the fence post at the back of the school. It picked the small bird clean to the bones. Hogan wondered about bird heaven. One moment the small bird is flitting about the sky, and the next moment he's dinner. Is the hawk a bad guy or just the deliverer? Was the bird's life meaningful or senseless? He closes the lid, and as he turns back, he watches a small group of parishioners walking down the church steps. The men are in coats and ties, and the women wear dresses. Suddenly, he hears gunshots and sees the parishioners duck. He knows instinctively and runs to the church as fast as his gimpy hip will allow. That's what Hogan remembers.

§

Tinker scratches on the screen door wanting to be let out after checking on the boy and the two women inside. Hogan stands and steps to the door. Tinker ambles out and sprawls on the porch. The old dog makes an old dog sound before quickly falling asleep. Hogan hesitates. He sidesteps to the window and looks in, but Esch has moved out of the kitchen, so he can't see her. He turns around and moves to the edge of the porch where he can see the starry sky. These things happen, these terrible things, and there is no explanation. It's not God's doing, but only He may understand why. This is completely and utterly irrational. Things like this leave scars. Hogan remembers.

CHAPTER 6

Nobody treats Fulton's head wound at the bar. A few of the men pick him up, toss him into the back of a pickup truck, and drop him at Morvid's house, at his house. They lay him on the porch, ring the doorbell, and leave. He hadn't known about the shooting earlier in the day, so anyone feeling sorry for him would have been mistaken. Those who know him well never feel sorry for Fulton. He has spent this Sunday in the forest up near the Little Prince Mine where he was hired to mend a fence, but he started drinking early and never got to the repairs. He slept in the late afternoon and into the evening and then drove straight to The Jungle when he returned to town. Nobody in the bar told him his son had been at the church. Only the stranger bothered to strike up a conversation, and he got beaten for his loose talk. When Fulton drinks, violence often ensues.

Morvid drags Fulton into the foyer and tends to his bloody head. It isn't particularly bad; certainly nothing to seek a doctor about. Morvid inflicted worse on his grandson when he raised him, and Fulton has inflicted his share of pain on Morvid over the past decade. Fulton is a strong man, manual labor strong, and the tallest of the Trees. Morvid bragged about his grandson's athletic accomplishments in high school, excused his fights as youthful aggression, and breathed a sigh of relief when Fulton joined the Army and headed off to Vietnam. Unfortunately, he came back to Eagle Canyon. Morvid doesn't try to wake Fulton, doesn't try to tell him that his son has been at a mass shooting. Morvid leaves Fulton on the floor with a pillow under his head and returns to the kitchen to finish his coffee. The old man never imagined that he would still be raising a boy this late in life.

Three days earlier, the Tree family that still lives in Eagle Canyon observed Morvid's eightieth birthday. Hogan did not come. Morvid sat at the table and picked at the remains of the cake that Burelle bought at the grocery store, chocolate with carrot frosting. Morvid teased Random that his red hair had dyed the frosting. Morvid wishes Burelle and Random were home tonight, at his house, but they have chosen to go to Hogan's house after the shooting and stay there. Burelle wouldn't feel safe if Fulton wasn't sober, and he hasn't been in weeks. She needs to stay with Hogan for now. Still, Morvid wishes that he could hold Random on his lap and read him a story before bed, to reassure himself that his great-grandson is okay. Morvid pours himself a glass of water from the faucet and sits at the table. Nights, he thinks, so different from the days. Nights are full of regrets, full of stirrings. The days have a routine, but the nights bring remorse.

At some time well past two in the morning, Morvid goes to bed. His wife Danver died in the early sixties, when her heart wore out, and since then, he sleeps alone. Actually, they hadn't slept in the same bed for more than a decade at the end of their marriage. They had been married for forty-seven years, and she was about the age he is now. Those last years, she seemed more like his older sister or aunt, certainly not his wife. He doesn't miss her at all. She was a mean, nasty old woman for a good part of her life; mean to him, to Hogan, to Fulton, to the whole world.

§

Fulton is still passed out when Morvid arises, but Fulton somehow managed to get to the couch after Morvid went to bed. He checks his grandson's head. The large bandage has some blood on it that has leaked onto the couch pillow, but Fulton's head doesn't seem swollen. Morvid puts coffee on the stove and walks outside to collect the Denver newspaper. The headline reads as he suspected it would: "Three Shot to Death in Eagle Canyon." The story tells the grizzly details, the facts of which he is already acutely aware. There are pictures of the church and of Hogan carrying Random away, covered with blood. By chance, a Post photographer had been visiting friends in Eagle Canyon when the shooting occurred and took the first pictures, the photos that will be emblazoned in people's minds for years to come. Morvid knows everyone involved: the teacher, the teenagers, the little boys, the killer, the police chief, the minister, and all their families. They are all part of the Eagle Canyon extended family, and Morvid does not understand this.

Around ten Fulton comes into the kitchen rubbing his head and smiling. "Kicked his ass before I got cold-cocked." He pours himself a cup and sits down opposite Morvid. "What's that you're reading?" Morvid rotates the front page, shoves it over the table, and puts his finger on Hogan's picture. Fulton leans into the paper and reads. He says nothing until he finishes the entire story. Morvid waits and watches Fulton's expressions. When he finishes the account, he sits back, nods his head, and lets out a grunt. He looks at Morvid. "Do you suppose you might have told me earlier?"

Morvid senses the rising anger in Fulton and proceeds slowly. "You weren't near a phone, so I couldn't call. I went looking but didn't know where to look. You weren't at The Jungle when this all happened. I even checked back around ten, but you still weren't there." Morvid's legs tense under the table.

"You should have kept looking, checked back at the bar. I'm his father, you know. He's mine." Fulton stands and Morvid flinches. "I'm not going to hit you, old man. Is Random at Hogan's?"

"Yeah. Burelle's there too. Hogan won't let you in. He might shoot you if you try." Morvid doesn't want to challenge Fulton, but he thinks it best to remind him of something he already knows, that Hogan's house is off limits.

"That would be another headline for the paper. 'Father shoots son whose son was shot in shooting.' You'd have some explaining to do." Fulton looks through his grandfather as if the old man doesn't exist. A moment later Fulton takes the last drink of his coffee, points at Morvid, swears, and leaves.

Tears form in the corners of Morvid's eyes, as often happens to old men. He gets up and goes to the phone, dials, and waits. A lifetime in Eagle Canyon, but yesterday and the rest of the week will be some of the hardest days.

CHAPTER 7

The journalism student begins the next session by asking Morvid to clarify a previous point. "Did being a soldier make you feel more American in some way? I mean, you said that your father left Europe to avoid conscription, but you're saying war was a great adventure. You speak almost fondly about it."

The old man nods and smiles. "Before the war I was an outsider; my family was seen as different, I guess. Coming home as a veteran, especially one who saw action in the great American battles, let me into the club. It granted me admission to the American Club, and that was a great gift."

Morvid wants to talk more about the war, but the student moves him ahead to his life in Eagle Canyon. The student believes the old man could ramble on every day of the summer. What is it about war that overrides every other memory for all men, thinks the student?

"When I returned from the war, from France, I refused to follow in my Pap's footsteps and become a miner. I got work at the bank and started a career. America in the Twenties was booming, and I wanted in. Danver never wanted to talk about the war or my extended time in Europe after the armistice. She was smart enough to know that soldiers can't be held accountable for every action they partake in during war. Soldiers kill other soldiers, and when they're not doing that, they have to occupy their time. So, we had a good marriage. I bought a house up on the side of the hill not far from here that we lived in for most of the decade. The kids were all born there; Hogan was my first. He was a pistol at first, always running around. I'd find him all across town doing something. Storeowners would call me to come and get him. The fence around the house couldn't contain him, he was just so curious. He loved the hills and river, especially that river. Danver always thought he'd drown, a young boy playing in that river, especially when it was flowing fast in spring. But he was just being a boy, not being afraid of nothing.

"About the only thing I thought about was getting even with the man who murdered Pap. I talked to people in the know about what went down and pretty much learned that Pap had merely confronted Davis about his boys destroying our cabin. None of the Davis boys were around. They had gone to war too, and Davis's family would suffer hard. Two of the boys wouldn't return from the fighting, killed in France at St. Mihiel. Another was injured and all messed up in the head and stayed at a hospital back east, and the last Davis boy came home and died of influenza with so many others, like my brother, before I got back.

"The best I could ascertain was that Pap confronted Davis on his front porch, and an argument ensued, and Davis went into the house for his gun and killed Pap right there on the front steps. Pap died in Davis's front yard. Davis went back inside and left Pap there for others to find and deal with. I couldn't let that image go; it was a powerful image in my brain. I guess what I'm saying is that I didn't care about Davis's other problems. He killed Pap and I wanted revenge.

"I had Pap's old shotgun and .22, but I really wanted a revolver, so I sold Pap's two rifles for one. I've got a lot of guns now. Anyway, when I got the pistol, I went to where Davis worked over at the smelter and pointed it in his face. I wanted to scare him. I told him that he had to take responsibility for his sons' behaviors in destroying our cabin, and that he couldn't get away with just killing Pap and leaving him in the yard like a cur. He stared at me with a blank face; didn't say anything. Some of the other men at the smelter got me out of there, and I went home, but I had shown him. I still wanted to kill him though.

"A couple of days later or maybe a week, I can't be sure since it was over fifty years ago, old man Davis came to the bank with his rifle looking for me. The bank guard shot him dead right there in the lobby. You can't bring a loaded rifle into a bank without consequences. It was the end of the Davis clan in Eagle Canyon. The rest of the family just vanished, moved somewhere else.

"That's when I decided to rebuild the cabin. It took me two summers to complete, but I built it on the same spot where Pap and I had originally put it, right there where the ashes of the first one were, sort of like a Phoenix. I tried to make it as similar as I could remember, and when it was done, I hung the only picture of Pap that I had out there on the wall over the eating table. It's still there today. It's our family place. All the children loved it when they were growing up. That cabin contains the souls of the Trees. It's our shrine."

The student holds up his hand for Morvid to wait. "When did you tell your son, Hogan, right, about your father's murder? Or did you ever tell him?"

"Oh yeah, when he was a little older, maybe around seven or eight. It was part of the larger lesson that fathers are responsible for their children, that Davis should have managed his sons better, or at least owned up to their misbehavior."

"How did Hogan take it?"

"Fathers tell their sons lots of things as they're growing up. You never know what sticks and what doesn't. We never talked about it after that. What's done is done." This last sentence is said almost like a canon of faith.

"One more thing before we wrap up today's session," says the student. "It's difficult to keep up with the names in your family. Yours, Fulton, Hogan, Random, your wife's. They're all so strange."

Morvid laughs. "Your professor wants a normal American family, and in some ways, we are, but I like to think the Trees are unique . . . unlike any other family. Let the names slowly roll off your tongue. Morvid Tree. Hogan Tree. Fulton Tree. Random Tree. Then substitute a common name like Bob. Bob Tree. Or Jim. Jim Tree. I don't think so. I will admit that Danver is a little weird though. Since the immigration people messed up the original family name so long ago, we've been having fun with names ever since."

CHAPTER 8

When the eastern sky begins to show a little morning, Hogan rises from the wicker chair to walk the perimeter of his yard with Tinker. Tinker wanders too, a private dog, so she makes good company for Hogan. She arrived on the back step begging for food a half-dozen years earlier and stayed. She keeps her distance from strangers as if she had been abused as a pup. Tinker likes Burelle and Random though; she senses goodness in them, and now questions Hogan several times to ask why they are sitting up so late in the house. Tinker also wants to know about the short lady. "It's okay, missy, they just need some safe time alone. Randy got a little hurt, but he's going to be fine. You and me'll just keep an eye out for a while. Okay?" He explained this to Tinker several times in the night, but the old dog can't remember. He releases Tinker to go inside again and check for herself; she returns satisfied and sits down on the porch. Hogan is on guard for his son. Fulton knows better than to come around, knows he isn't welcome, but the unique circumstances of the day might change what Fulton knows. Since he didn't show up at the church or call about Random, Hogan is certain his son was out drinking somewhere, unaware of the shooting. Alcohol has always fueled his actions, thinks Hogan. Alcohol and drugs, but they aren't the engine.

Before the sun comes up, Deputy Esch leaves. She visits briefly with Hogan and then walks to her squad car, which is parked down the block so as not to draw attention to where Burelle and Random are staying. The Denver press wants interviews. Eventually, they will find Random, "the brave little boy who tried to comfort his Sunday school teacher," and deliver a piece of him for their readers. Hogan wants to delay that process for as long as he can, but he understands the news value of Randy, a cute, redheaded boy with his front teeth missing. Better that they interview Randy and Burelle than pester the families of the two slain teenagers.

After Esch leaves, Hogan goes in to fix breakfast. He will try to resume a normal routine for Random's life. Burelle has taken Random to the couch and lain down with him. When the bacon begins to sizzle, Randy comes in and hugs his grandfather around the waist. "Smells good, Grampa. Will there be enough for all of us?" It's a game Hogan and Random always play. Hogan will fry up four strips of bacon, and the boy will devour them all. Then Hogan will act surprised when he finds more strips to be cooked so everyone can have some.

"Are you doing all right, Randy? You had a pretty hard day yesterday." Hogan slides a kitchen stool over to the counter so that Random can help him cook. "Hand me that spatula, Randy, please."

"Yeah, Grampa, I'm okay. Do you know how Kevin and Marty are?"

"Deputy Esch said they will be fine. Kevin's going to have to wear a cast, but it's on his left arm, so his pitching arm is okay. I know Marty looked bad, but it was someone else's blood. He's okay like you." Hogan pauses to turn the bacon and then covers it with a mesh lid. "What else do you want with your bacon?"

"Maybe some cereal and orange juice. Mrs. Tuttle's dead, isn't she?" Random climbs off the stool and goes to the pantry for the box of Wheaties. He returns to his grandpa's side and leans against him.

Hogan squats to Random's eye level and places his strong hands on his grandson's upper arms. "Yes, Randy, she is. She saved you boys, but she couldn't save herself. That's the way she was, you know. I'm sorry you had to see all of that. It wasn't your fault in any way. I want you to know that."

"That boy didn't have to shoot her. She backed us into the corner and pushed us behind her. She told him she would help him if he gave her his gun. He had already shot the two big boys She wanted to help him even after that." Random's fingers are wiggling just inches in front of his grandfather's face.

"You don't have to talk about it if you're not ready to, you know." Hogan reaches up and takes both of Random's hands, folding them together inside his rough hands.

"No, Grampa. It's okay. Besides, mommy won't want to hear it. I have to protect her."

"You're a brave boy, Randy, but you don't have to protect anyone. Your mommy will want what's best for you. Did you know that she held you all last night to help make you feel better?"

Hogan looks past Random to where Burelle sits on the couch. She's been listening. She nods her approval to Hogan and smiles gently. Burelle has trained herself not to think about what if, but watching Hogan with Random tempts her. She sees where Random gets his fair complexion and puffy cheeks, his pointed chin and high forehead. She bites the inside of her lower lip, already calloused, and watches. Each time Hogan moves from the stove, he touches Random in a reassuring manner. He should have been a wonderful father, but how does one explain Fulton? Random has spent lots of nights in this house, but she never has. Despite her lack of sleep and yesterday's shooting, she isn't tired, unlike most of her mornings.

"Is the bacon burning?" asks Random. His grandpa tousles his hair and turns to the stove.

§

After breakfast Burelle and Hogan sit on the back porch drinking coffee while Random brushes his teeth inside. Hogan finally speaks. "That's a fine boy you've raised." He allows his words to sink in. "Morvid's house isn't a nurturing place, but you've created your little nest and protected Randy from its evils. I respect you for that." Hogan's words mask his guilt. The big house had a different feel when Fulton was in the Army and nine-thousand miles away. No one would confuse Morvid with an affectionate great-grandfather, but there was a quiet, relaxed calm in his house when Burelle and Random moved in. They certainly needed help, needed structure, and they got it for three years. Then Fulton returned and ordered Burelle out. Morvid convinced Fulton that if Burelle left, no one would be there to watch over Random, to tend to his daily needs, so she was forced to stay, not in the big house, but in a two-room addition attached to the east side of the house. When Randy told Hogan about Fulton's late-night visits, about the screaming and fighting, Hogan confronted his son in the big house. Hogan jammed a pistol into Fulton's belly and warned him to keep his hands off Burelle and Randy. He wanted to kill his son at that moment, and he scared himself at his ferociousness. It was the last time Hogan was in his father's house. The abuse seemed to have stopped, but Burelle and Random stayed.

"Thank you." Burelle keeps her eyes focused on the back yard, maybe watching Tinker run around. She avoids discussions about her relationship with Fulton and her living accommodations, but Hogan knows her plight better than anyone else, and occasionally, she will drop her guard. She knows his plight too. Morvid and Fulton never miss an opportunity to tell her about Hogan's failings—as a husband and a father, that all he is is a janitor, and a crazy one at that.

"What happened yesterday confuses me. A shooting at a church in this town. Makes no sense." Hogan pauses and Burelle waits, knowing there is more. He allows his thoughts to flow out slowly. "I think I understand violence that's personal, violence against someone who's harmed or threatened you, but this shooting seems without reason. A boy walks into a church and shoots people who've never harmed him. Seemed like a good boy. I don't get that." He holds his coffee near his mouth with both hands. "I worry about you, Burelle. You carry a heavy load, and this is one more bale of hay." Hogan reaches over and squeezes Burelle's forearm.

"I'm okay. I just wish Random didn't have to experience all of this. He didn't deserve yesterday."

"No one deserves that."

"No, no one." Burelle reaches over with her right hand and covers Hogan's hand on her forearm.

Random bounces outside, letting the screen door slam behind him. He grins to show his mother his teeth for inspection. She nods in approval which releases Random to play with Tinker in the yard.

"We're a strange bunch of people, aren't we?" says Hogan.

"The Trees or Eagle Canyon?"

"I was referring to Eagle Canyon. We've always known about the family."

"Are people in every small town like us?" asks Burelle.

"Mostly, I guess. Strange might be the wrong word." Hogan pauses. "There have to be towns that are normal somewhere." He pauses again. "We collect in our spots of comfort, in restaurants or coffee shops, share meals, watch Little League baseball games, attend school activities, and think this is the world." He sips his coffee. "Maybe this is normal, and that yesterday will be the one day in all of our little town's history that stands apart. We'll all go back to feeling comfortable here."

"I never have. It's not my world. I'm from here, but still, I'm an outsider." Random drags Tinker onto the porch by her collar. The dog settles next to Hogan, and Random climbs onto his mom's lap. Hogan pulls his hand off Burelle's arm and scratches Tinker, while Burelle readjusts her son on her lap before continuing with her thought. "There has to be a normal town for Random and me. Tell me about your wife. Why did she leave?"

Hogan runs his hand through the white hair that remains on his head. Burelle has always thought that Hogan looks older than his age. He bites the inside of his mouth. "She wasn't from here, so she had a place to go back to. She went home to her family in New Zealand . . . where she was safe. Burelle, she left because of Fulton. He hurt her just like he used to hurt you." He pauses. "She couldn't understand why I sent her away alone. She resisted. She does now though. She's a good woman, and I wouldn't allow her to be damaged by this any longer."

Both go quiet for a moment, and then Hogan adds, "I didn't know if I could ever love anyone again until I carried Randy out of the church. And then I found that I did. It was just buried under so much pain—and shit. I found that you mattered to me too, because you are Randy's mother—and a very good mother throughout these difficult years."

"Thank you, Hogan. Random is part Tree and part me. My

hope is that his genetic code from my side will overcome that of the Trees. Still though, you are a Tree, Hogan, and that's good for Random. My parents were no angels. Random's future is not guaranteed, that's for sure."

§

Robbie Hollins lies on his cot with his face to the wall. He doesn't speak, hasn't spoken since his arrival yesterday, but it seems not from anger or a plan, but as if he checked out of life immediately after being transported from the church to the jail. He's abnormally slender, not especially tall, and pale of skin, with furtive eyes. Police Chief Russo has not allowed anyone access to Robbie except his mother and Doctor Mason. As they do with Random Tree, the press maintains a vigil outside the police station hoping to get a photo or a tidbit for a story. Colorado wants to know. So does Chief Russo.

Russo rolls his desk chair to the front of the cell and sits. He excuses the part time deputy who maintains a constant watch over this most important prisoner. Russo is a heavy man, an experienced chief, a local. He joined the Army after high school, served as an M.P. in Korea, tried his hand at big-city police work in Chicago, but couldn't deal with the heat and politics there, or the common gun violence in the poorer sections, so he returned to Eagle Canyon in the late fifties. He wanted to work where he believed he could make a difference, in a town where he could protect the citizens. More than the mayor, more than the high school principal, more than the men who live on the hill, Russo runs Eagle Canyon. It's his town and he watches over it. Russo's butt fills the chair. He hasn't slept since the shooting.

"Son, I need to ask you some questions so I can complete this paperwork." Robbie doesn't stir, but Russo continues. "Robbie, I've known you all of your life, and you've never been in trouble, so what happened? What caused you to go crazy all of a sudden?" After each question he waits, giving the prisoner time to respond, but Robbie keeps his face hidden from the police chief. "You probably don't know yourself, do you?" Russo sighs, leans forward, and puts his hands on the bars from his chair. "Reverend Chamberlain says you were in church, that you sat with your mother near the back. He didn't see you after the service. Were the guns in your car, or did you drive home to get them?" Russo waits. He doesn't really know anything, but he throws out provocative questions, hoping for a reaction. "My guess is you drove your mother home and got the guns then, huh?" The chief waits longer this time. A court-appointed lawyer is scheduled to visit Robbie later, but he hasn't called or shown up at the station. He'll advise Robbie not to say anything. The boy was read his rights in the patrol car at church and then again at the station in front of two officers and the dispatcher. The part about "the right to remain silent" hasn't been necessary.

The police chief swivels his chair to the left and asks, "Did your mom help plan this in any way?"

Without turning, Robbie says softly, but emphatically, "No."

"Did she buy you the guns, Robbie? Were they your guns or your mom's?" Robbie doesn't answer. "I see her out at the range frequently. Polite lady. I've watched her with the nine-millimeter, but I've never seen her with an AK-47. Where did you get it, Robbie?" Russo pushes back, stands, and walks to the barred window. He looks out onto the alley and waits. In time he saunters back to the cell and rests his shoulder against the door. "Your silence won't protect you or your mother, son. If she helped you obtain the guns and the ammunition and knowingly acquiesced in the killings, then she has some culpability. Three people that I knew well are dead, and I'll be damned if I'm gonna let that go."

Robbie starts to turn over but stops and rolls back toward the wall. He pulls the sheet over his head and curls up into a fetal position. He won't hear another word from the police chief; he travels back three months in time.

§

Robbie evaluates himself in front of the full-length mirror that hangs on the coat closet door in the entryway. Dressed in his black graduation gown, he readjusts his mortarboard, trying to get just the right slant. The yellow tassel is a hindrance. He will walk into the gym alone at the end of the procession since none of his class-mates chose him as a partner. If he's lucky, he'll get paired with another single for balance. Names will not be called in alphabetical order, but by order of entry in the procession. He will be last, almost as an afterthought.

He's not tough enough, he thinks. He tilts his head for effect, but to see how he appears, he has to maintain eye contact with himself. Eye contact scares him; it gives him away. He shakes his head slightly, opens the closet, and steps in. He picks up his mother's Winchester rifle and then closes the door. In the darkness he assumes the port arms position. What he guards is difficult to ascertain, but he stands motionless—like a sentry or a statue in a black gown. A shard of light enters from beneath the door allowing him to train his eyes in the darkness.

Later that afternoon he hears his mother come home, but he doesn't relax his position. She will come to him; she knows the drill. She will knock first; he'll give her permission to open the door; she'll ask how his day went; and then she will say, "At ease." He'll nod at his mother, put the rifle down, and come out of the closet. Today, she wants to take graduation photos before the weekend ceremony. She worries about him. He wishes he could pose with the Winchester.

§

"I'm pretty sure your mom didn't know what you were planning, but she did allow you access to the pistol. I just don't know about the automatic rifle though." The police chief doesn't know; he's not bluffing. Then he remembers something. "Did you buy that rifle at the gun show last month? Without waiting for a response that isn't forthcoming, Russo returns to his desk. He picks up the phone, cradles it between his ear and shoulder, spins his rolodex, and dials a number. When the secretary on the other end answers, the police chief asks, "At the gun show in Eagle Canyon in July, do you have a record of a sale of a 47 to anyone? Would there be a receipt somewhere?"

CHAPTER 9

The young journalist turns the page of his spiral notebook, flips on his recorder, and looks up at Morvid, indicating his readiness to continue. The Sunday school shooting has still not occurred, but Elvis Presley died two days ago. The old man rubs his mouth with his left hand and goes on.

"My son Hogan Tree was born in 1922. My wife already had three children from another man before she met me, so that made four. Did I tell you that she was several years older than me? Danver and I had two more daughters after that, making for a pretty big household, and eventually we needed a bigger house. Late in the decade, we moved here, and this is where I've lived ever since. Right here in this Victorian. Hogan was a fine boy from the get-go: smart, good looking, and active. He was the pick of the litter, that's for sure. Eagle Canyon was in a good place in the Twenties too, and my job at the bank paid well. The only problem was that my wife had a temper, and she took it out on Hogan and the two younger girls, never on her own kids. She was especially hard on Hogan. It was like she never considered him as one of hers. There were her kids and my kids, three of each. No matter. I sort of divided the family the same way. She'd get on me to discipline him too, so Hogan got whipped a bunch. He never seemed to mind, though, just took it in stride. I think that bothered Danver. I don't know if your professor wants you to interview anyone else in the Tree family, but Hogan is the exception. He's not like me or Pap or Fulton. Somewhere, he got misdirected. You might ask him why.

"When Hogan was about ten or twelve, he fell in with reading and began to change. Before that, he and I spent a lot of time together, but after that, he was off on his own and didn't spend as much time at home. This house was a busy, noisy place, and I think he found it distracting. It's funny that a young boy would spend so much time with his face in a book and not play as much baseball or football, especially since he was good at both. I always blamed his sixth-grade teacher for that. I let him have it too, at a conference once, told him that Hogan would have plenty of time to read when he got older, but that he was a boy and needed to be with the other boys doing kid stuff. I don't remember that teacher's name, but he looked like a queer, and I didn't want my boy hanging around him. Ran him out of town, but it didn't stop Hogan from reading, and he never was as interested in hanging out with me after that. It wasn't right for that teacher to take away Hogan's childhood.

"When I grew up in Eagle Canyon, families tended to stay in their own neighborhoods, but with the boom and more prosperity, that started to change. Then the Depression hit, and some of the old families collected together again. You could see it everywhere; people clung to their own. I was lucky though. The Depression didn't take my job. Some of the men at the bank had to move on, but not me. Each time one of the men got laid off, I moved up, and by the time war broke out in Europe, I was a vice-president of the bank. This Tree from Poland had made it in America.

"Hogan was a smart boy in high school. The top student, if I remember right, but for sure the top boy in his class. Good athlete too. I made him play sports, and he did all right. I'm sure if you asked him, he'd say I done right to make him play. He never got into any trouble. He didn't drink with his friends; he just focused on his books and classes. He wanted to go to college and be a teacher, and he earned a scholarship to your university up in Boulder. But the war in Europe had started, and it was just a matter of time before it took another Tree."

CHAPTER 10

After leaving Morvid's house, Fulton drives unannounced to Denver to see his current girlfriend, but she isn't there. He doesn't think about Random, only that nobody bothered to tell him about the shooting in town. That isn't right, and someone will pay. He returns to Eagle Canyon and to the church out of curiosity, but the police presence keeps him at a distance. Scores of onlookers line the sidewalk behind the tape barriers. A small gathering of out-of-town ministers in cassocks kneel in prayer. Fulton walks the perimeter, nods at a few people, but engages in no conversation of substance. He spots Esch with Chief Russo near a side entrance of the church. She holds what looks like an artist's brush, whisking it along a door frame. Just a girl trying to be more important than a girl should, he thinks, trying to fill a role designed for a man. Patrol officer, he sneers, more like the local meter maid. Each time he sees Esch, he wants to put her back in high school, back at the cabin, back to when he controlled her every move. Only her new job and fancy uniform protects her.

Fulton decides to shave his beard. Maybe, he thinks, people don't recognize me; don't see me as Random's dad, and that's why nobody's asking about my son's condition. The beard does cover his skin blotches from Vietnam, however, and makes him look tougher. Maybe I'll keep the beard a little longer.

"How's your boy," asks a man from behind.

The question seems to startle Fulton, but it's not the question. He turns to find Hogan's sunken eyes staring deep into his eyes. Fulton takes a half-step backward and regains his confident look. "Nice photo in the newspaper, Pop. I see you didn't have anything to say to them."

Hogan maintains his glare and gives his head a half shake. "Don't you want to know about Randy?"

"They couldn't hurt my boy. Us Trees are too damn tough. Besides, Morvid told me all about it last night when I came back from the job at the mine. I knew he was safe with you and Burelle. You two are making a sissy out of him."

Hogan takes a step into his son and intensifies his glare. "You watch out on this one, Fulton. Randy had a time of it yesterday while you were out drunk somewhere. You do anything stupid to him or Burelle, and I'll come see you." He holds his position for long enough to break Fulton's posture, then turns and walks away.

Fulton watches his father distance himself. He wants to run after him and jump on his back or punch him in the kidney. What gives him the right? When Hogan turns the corner and is out of sight, Fulton looks back to Esch. That bitch has turned everyone in town against me, he thinks. He turns to walk up the hill to his house but decides on a beer at The Jungle. Morvid would just probe him with questions that aren't his business. He's like everyone else in this pitiful town.

§

Roberta has heard Fulton's laments dozens of times, but she's paid to listen to her customers' stories each time she serves up another drink. Besides, Morvid makes sure his son's bar tab is always paid up. Like most of the young men who frequent the bar, Fulton has plans. He won't be staying in this town long, just long enough to save a few dollars before heading out to greener pastures. Roberta laughs at that phrase. Greener pastures. Fulton uses it frequently, "From Eagle Canyon to Greener Pastures," as if it's another town's name somewhere far from here. Roberta likes Fulton when he's not drunk; nobody likes Fulton when he is drunk, but he buys others' beers, tips well, and keeps the bar lively. She slept with him when he returned from his war, but they both moved on. She clubbed him over the head last night with the shotgun that is kept beneath the bar, but he'll never find out about that. She won't tell and neither will The Jungle's patrons. Chief Russo knows, however.

She slides a beer in front of Fulton. "Are you doing okay, dude?"

"Yeah, babe. My head hurts a bit, but I'll survive."

"That head is too hard to be seriously damaged, besides, if the VC couldn't kill you, neither could a little bump on the noggin." Roberta leans over the bar revealing her ample cleavage to Fulton. "How's your boy?"

"He didn't get hurt. He's looking forward to leaving this town with me next spring." Fulton swallows a quarter of his beer and reaches for the bowl of pretzels. "He's a tough kid and deserves better than Eagle Canyon. I'm thinking we'll end up in Denver with my girlfriend, maybe one of the suburbs where people mind their own business."

"So, you'll be staying through the winter to bother me some more?" teases Roberta.

"Yeah, probably. We'll go sooner if things work out. I wouldn't want to just up and leave without telling you, though."

Roberta reaches over and touches Fulton's nose, straightens up, and smiles. She knows she'll be doing this dance with Fulton for years to come. He'll be like the middle-aged man at the end of the bar who's been planning to leave Eagle Canyon for Phoenix since LBJ was president. For him, it's not Greener Pastures, but Warmer Weather.

CHAPTER 11

Morvid lays out some family photos, grainy black and whites, for the student.

"World War II did strange things to Eagle Canyon. It took most of the young men, but in a funny way, it gave the town a purpose and energy. The women especially got involved in wartime activities to help the soldiers overseas. It also gave some of the unemployed miners a new life, because jobs opened up. The mine was important to America's war effort. Hogan quit college and enlisted in the Navy. I didn't want him to go to college anyway; I could have gotten him a job at the bank, but he was set on getting a degree. English, if you can believe that. Wanted to be a teacher. That's probably why he ended up where he is today; couldn't get that college degree. He's a janitor over at the school.

"Anyway, we followed the war every day. It was easy to do; that was all the news was about. The war against the Japs was our war. That's what got us into the whole thing anyway, the Japs attacking Pearl. I was proud of Hogan for going to fight them. I told everyone in town about the job my boy was doing. He served on a boat, away from the real killing. He didn't see war like me or Fulton did. I think that might be why he doesn't understand his boy that well. We were all proud of our sons. It took a while though. The Japs were kicking us pretty good for that first year, until Midway. Then, we got 'em.

"Hogan couldn't write to us much during the war. I knew he was a gunner on a destroyer; I think that's what damaged his hearing and made him so self-conscious after the war. He was wounded, shot through the hip by a Jap plane. He spent time in Australia after one of his boats sunk before getting assigned to a new one. That's where he met Gertie, although she was from New Zealand. I forget whether he met her in Darwin or Sydney. Doesn't matter, sometime during the war while he was still in the Navy, they got married. He came back to get out of the Navy, and when he did, he left for New Zealand to get her. They stayed there for a couple of years, but eventually made it back around '48 or '49, I think, maybe in '50. He bought the house where he lives now a few blocks from here. I offered to have them live with us, but they wanted their own place. You could talk to him about the Trees, but he doesn't say much. He mostly talks to himself.

"Gertie and I didn't get along too good; she kind of had a will that took Hogan away from me and the family. Gertie especially didn't like Danver. Gertie and Hogan didn't start a family right away. Hogan just said it wasn't the right time. He said he wanted to get the war out of his system, to not lay any of it on babies. He also took a few college courses too, while Gertie worked. That girl could ride horses like no one you ever saw, and she was able to find work on a ranch up the valley. There was always something about the war or his life in New Zealand that he never told me, kept it a secret. Those two were as close as any couple you ever saw, but they kept everyone else at a distance.

"Fulton was born in '53, easy to remember, because the Korean War ended that year. He was their only kid."

CHAPTER 12

Before returning to Morvid's house, Burelle again bathes Random thoroughly, hoping to wash away entirely the blood, bits of flesh, gunpowder odor, and memories of the previous day. She sees her son as a baby this morning, not as an eight-year-old boy. Random is tired, like a child who has spent twenty-four hours at the amusement park and can no longer hold his head up. She moves the washcloth slowly, methodically, over Random's body, using her free hand to raise his arms or bend his ears in order to reach each spot of his skin. She finds traces of dried blood in the cracks of his ears and under his fingernails, and even some on his eyelids. When she finishes, she drains the tub and refills it, not wanting the first water to leave any residue on that pure skin. After drying him, she wraps him in a beach towel and carries him to the couch to nap again. She goes to the laundry room to put his clothes in the dryer. Random is asleep when she returns. She takes an afghan from a corner chair and gently covers him.

Her turn. Burelle removes her clothes and steps into the tub for a shower, allowing the spray to engulf her body as if a huge pitcher of water is being slowly poured over her head. With her eyes closed, she sees Mrs. Tuttle. Thank you, Margaret. Burelle leans forward, placing her forehead against the wall and mixes her tears with the shower stream. After a few minutes, she straightens and turns off the shower. She towels off and re-dresses in the same clothes, except for a blue work shirt that she has borrowed from Hogan.

The dryer still has twenty minutes left, so she sits with Random on the couch, fingering his hair and face. Burelle is confused. Violence has been a part of her life, but she always accepted a part of the responsibility. Yesterday, though, violence was directed at Random from outside her being, in God's house, by a former altar boy. What could I have done? She shudders. Violence is a disease or a curse, and this family I belong to has it. She thinks back to Random's birth. He came out at four pounds even, but healthy in every other way. The nurses nicknamed him Squirt until he took on the legal name of Random. His eyes matched Fulton's, blue; not like her dark eyes. She wanted to name him Patrick John, but Fulton came to the hospital on the second day and put Random on the birth certificate. Fulton didn't visit her; he just looked at Random through the glass, nodded to Morvid, signed papers that he was the father, and left. Burelle wasn't even allowed to name her own son, a son that wasn't going home to a father, but to an alcoholic grandmother in a trailer home. Morvid paid the hospital costs, and Esch came to drive her and Random home. Home. It's a foreign word to her, and without one of her own, she feels a lack of security, both for herself and Random.

The dryer buzzes. Burelle slides off the couch to retrieve Random's clothes and take him home. Home is what Morvid called it when he called earlier. He promised to keep the press at bay, or at least outside the fence. More importantly, he told her that Fulton wasn't there. Burelle and Random live at Morvid's house, but not with them. They live in the house; she and Random occupy the guest portion. It contains one bedroom, a bathroom, a small kitchen-dining area, and a separate entrance. It's similar to a guest cottage, only attached to the main house. Guests. Random Tree and Burelle Oakley. Fulton laughs frequently that Random is the result of one random night of drinking with Burelle and Esch, and brags about it to anyone who will listen. Fulton never married the mother of his son, never wanted to, and never will, but he wants control over Random. Morvid suggested the living arrangement, and he believes that it works out.

Burelle lies about the arrangement. The few people in Eagle Canyon who don't know Fulton, but see a bruised woman, believe she's a closet drunk with seizures who falls down frequently. Fulton and Morvid offer that story. At the hospital two years back, a counselor told her domestic abuse was more about power and control than violence. Burelle shot back that the lady had never been hit with a fist in the stomach, been slapped repeatedly, been dragged around the house by her hair, or forced to have sex with a drunken man. Then she stormed out to pretend again that she fell down some steps after having too much to drink, to be silent in the world of make believe.

Burelle and Random walk the alley way back from Hogan's in order to avoid exposure. Eagle Canyon is a long, narrow town. It shares the canyon with the river that has given the town its livelihood since the Colorado gold rush began in 1859. But no longer. Eagle Canyon is now a mountain tourist town with lots of restaurants and curio shops. Main Street is the spine with a slight bit of scoliosis near the elementary school where the river bends slightly. No side street is longer than four blocks long, and many of them are only one lane wide. The park straddles the river; the ball fields were built on the opposite side of the interstate where the construction trucks carved out an area for parking when the highway was enlarged into an interstate in the fifties; the downtown lies in the exact middle of the town, a quaint seven blocks of brick buildings restored from the previous century. Before eight in the morning and after three in the afternoon, school children walk Main Street on their way to and from classes at the elementary or high school. Eagle Canyon is an intimate town where nearly everyone knows everyone else, or at least is aware of everyone.

Burelle and Random enter Morvid's yard from the hill side, through the back fence. Inside her portion she knocks on the wall that separates the two families to let Morvid know she's back. Morvid raps twice to respond. He doesn't come over, instead he goes to the front door to talk to the two reporters who wait by the gate.

Monday, August 22, 1977, the day after The Church Shooting. Please, God, thinks Burelle, don't allow yesterday to define Random's life. Give me a path to guide my son out of this mess, a way to make his life normal again. Let me carry his burden, but don't make him struggle with such a memory. She quickly returns to her basic belief about God's role in her life: He hasn't paid much attention before, and she doesn't expect Him to intervene now. Still, maybe He watched over Random and Kevin and Marty, but she wonders how their spirits will react to this violence over time. She pushes the flowered curtain aside to check on the reporters. Morvid talks to them, gesturing with both palms up, arms extended. They are dressed casually, both with long hair, and one with a beard. Neither looks threatening. Burelle decides to take Random out to give them their story, and maybe that will satisfy them. Maybe then the healing can begin. She turns back to watch her son scoot a toy car around the table legs and wonders how much longer.

"Mmmmmmmmmmmmm." Random's voice doesn't sound much like a corvette engine, but Burelle knows.

"Honey, how would you feel about talking with the newspaper reporters who have been standing outside all day?"

"If you want me to, I will." Random doesn't look up, concerning himself only with the obstacles on the floor.

"I think if we do it today, then they'll go away, and you can start playing in the yard again. How would you like that?"

"Will you go with me?"

"Of course. You can take your car too. Anything they ask, you don't have to answer. When you've said all you want, just tug my hand, and I'll send them away. Would that be okay?" Burelle knows she will dread this more than Random, knows it is she who wants to get this part of the drama out of the way. School starts in two weeks, and if she can somehow give Random these last two weeks of summer vacation back, then maybe he can heal.

Random stands and goes to his mother. He takes her hand, smiles up at her, and says in his biggest boy voice, "Okay, Mom, let's do it."

As they approach the gate, Morvid turns in surprise. Burelle tells him it's okay, but not to leave. She speaks first to the reporters, giving them the ground rules; that they are not to persist in any line of questioning once Random indicates any reluctance in answering. "I know you have to do your thing, but please go easy." Then, she squats to her son to check his readiness. He reassures her and she kisses him on the cheek.

The bearded reporter reaches over and extends his hand to Random. "I'm glad to see you're okay. From all I've heard, you were quite brave. Can you tell me where you were when the boy with the rifle came in?"

"I was sitting with my two friends listening to Mrs. Tuttle. She was my second-grade teacher last year, and she was telling us who our teacher is going to be this year. Mrs. Clark. That's when Robbie came in."

"You knew him?" asks the reporter to the little boy.

"Yes. He works at the church sometimes. He's an altar boy like the two boys he shot, only a little older. He knows them both."

The reporter looks to the other newspaperman and shares the thought. Everyone in the church room knew one another. Burelle reaches for Random's hand, but he looks up to her and nods that he is fine to continue. She tries to place Robbie, to remember what he looks like, but can't. She never noticed him.

The second reporter asks, "Random, do you know why he shot the boys and your teacher?"

"No. He came in and asked Mrs. Tuttle where Pastor Chamberlain was. Before she could answer, one of the altar boys said he was still in the church. I don't think Robbie knew those two boys were in the room. He just turned and shot them when they answered his question. Then he shot them again. Mrs. Tuttle stood and pushed me and Kevin and Marty into the corner. That's when Robbie shot her."

"Is that when he left?"

"No, he still screamed about Pastor Chamberlain. Then, he looked at me and pointed the gun, but he just lowered it and left."

§

Later in the day, Random tells Chief Russo the same thing. Robbie wasn't there, and then he was. He wanted to know where Pastor Chamberlain was, but he only seemed to be talking to Mrs. Tuttle, and she wouldn't tell him. She kept telling him to put down the gun, and then she would help him. He didn't want to talk to anyone else, because when Bradley tried to tell him, he shot both of the older boys.

"What did you say to him so he wouldn't hurt you?" asks the police chief.

"I told him to go home."

"Why did you tell him that, Random?"

"I don't know. I guess I just knew he shouldn't be with us, with that gun. Isn't that where you're supposed to go when you aren't wanted anywhere else?"

For the rest of the afternoon, Random sleeps on the couch with his head in on his mother's lap.

§

Russo leaves hurriedly. The mortician can't deal with the crowd of families that has descended on the funeral home, especially with Billy Dunn's mother, who won't leave her son. She flew in from Seattle earlier in the day and came directly to the mortuary. Old Fred O'Malley refused to allow her in the embalming room, believing that he was protecting her from seeing the grotesque injuries to Billy's face. He also had concerns about the legal requirements for an autopsy. Mr. Dunn tried to calm his wife, but he is too distraught to be effective. He sits silent in the waiting room, while she screams obscenities and won't allow anyone to touch her. Bradley's parents tried to comfort her, as did Mrs. Tuttle's husband, but she will have none of it. "He's alone! He can't be alone during the transition! I need to be with him!"

When Russo enters, he shows concern, but he is firm. He asks no questions. He moves directly to Mrs. Dunn, puts his arm around the large woman and guides her into O'Malley's office where he tells her how the process will continue. "Fred and his two colleagues have to do this. It can't wait. They will work on Billy first. I'm going to escort you in to be with him. You'll have a stool to sit on, and you can be with him while they do their work." The big man purses his lips and swallows hard, all the while keeping the grieving mother's eyes locked into his. Then he pulls her into his body. "Arlene, I'll go in with you and stay for a while. Billy has some disturbing facial wounds that Fred will have to reconstruct. Can you let him do his work?"

Arlene Dunn pulls back. "I know. I've been warned. As long as I can be with him, I'll be able to handle it. I just can't leave him alone. I won't abandon him this week."

Russo puts his hands on her shoulders. "Fred was just trying to shield you."

"I know. I'm sorry."

"He understands; no need to apologize." He looks at her closely and tries to sense her strength. It is considerable. "If you're ready, we can go in now."

In the embalming room, while O'Malley and his colleagues work, Mrs. Dunn talks and sings softly to her son. As gruesome as the process appears, she accepts it. While her son's face is washed, shaved, wired, glued, clamped, waxed, and sewn, she holds his hand. Families grieve differently, believe differently. Mrs. Dunn believes that her son's soul floats in limbo and must not be allowed to be isolated at this time. Burial will release the soul to God. His body was destroyed by a senseless act committed by a crazy boy, but Robbie doesn't have the power to hurt Billy's soul. Arlene Dunn will deliver her son's soul to God.

In the waiting room, Margaret Tuttle's husband consoles Mr. Dunn, while her daughter huddles with Billy's three siblings on the carpeted floor. Bradley Arnold's parents shake hands with the other adults and quietly leave.

CHAPTER 13

Beginning on Monday and for the rest of the week, Chief Russo schedules Esch to watch Robbie Hollins lie in his cell or to cruise in her patrol car in front of the three boys' houses. The out-of-town reporters seem to have gotten what they needed from Random and gather at the Hiway 6 breakfast café to exchange notes on the shooting, but curiosity seekers still stroll by. Random's two friends have been released from the hospital, their wounds being a ricochet and some wood splinters. Neither was shot directly, contrary to the early reports. Rumors fly that Mrs. Tuttle took more than two bullets to protect the three boys. Some will want to rename a park or the elementary school in her honor. Fulton does not return to Morvid's house the entire time. Instead, he works and sleeps in the cabin at the lake.

For Hogan, work will be his therapy. He continues to prepare the school for the arrival of students just after Labor Day. He and the principal work these long hours so every detail under their control will be accounted for. They respect one another and are comfortable in the belief that they run the building, albeit each in his own way. Hogan buffs the hallways. He will do it again on Labor Day so that the floors will glisten on the morning the students come in to complete their registration and find their new rooms. First impressions. When he's done, Hogan helps at the high school to repair two weight racks loosened by the football team when they held their preseason fundraiser on Saturday, the day before the shooting. If he could only convince the coach to make his athletes take off their cleats before they come into the gym after practice, the cleanup would be easier for his colleagues. After the weight room,

Hogan scrubs the carpet in the counseling office. He put this task late on his schedule, after late-registering students were gone, so it would have the evening and night to dry. On this Monday school is closed. Teachers are appearing more frequently to prepare their own rooms for the fall semester, although none will be in today. Bulletin boards, textbooks, lesson plans: there are a multitude of tasks for them. Hogan can count on a handful of the most dedicated to be in school each day as the fall semester approaches. Kaufman and Mireles at the elementary school, and Rowe, Clark, and old man Lawrence have already begun their year, even though there is no pay for these days. Hogan has a deep respect for teachers; after all, he wanted to be one once, a long time ago before his hearing problems arose, before he understood he couldn't be out front

At the end of the day, Hogan returns to check every outside door at the elementary school to ensure the building's security and to prevent vandalism. It is also his own way to monitor the little things that might need repair in the future, like sitting with one's son at bedtime and asking how his day went and getting a sense of his feelings and dreams. Hogan missed the signs in his own son.

Whitman Elementary School in Eagle Canyon is centrally located, not far from anyone who lives within the city proper. Hogan always walks to school, to work. He owns a car, but he puts very few miles on it anymore. Gertie picked it out, a station wagon. It was her car, and he takes good care of its maintenance, but since she left, except for that one period, it stays mostly in the garage. Working on it is a hobby and a way to get in touch with his wife. She liked the vanilla scent that he hung from the rearview mirror, and Hogan replaces that scent each time he cleans the interior of her car. Twelve years and vanilla still brings her back. After work Hogan walks home in the dark. On this Monday night, Esch is parked near his house, in front of Kevin's home. He taps on the window and she nods, reassuring him that things are okay. Hogan doesn't know if she is physically strong enough to stop any real threat, but he does know she would step out and do her damnedest to try. Hogan likes Esch. He always has. He once hoped she could make a difference for Burelle, but even she couldn't. Once Burelle moved in with Morvid, she became isolated, and she and Esch drifted apart. That happens after high school, and Esch was on the move. It's been good to see them reclaim their friendship in the months since Esch returned and was hired on at the police department. Hogan long ago gave up on the naïve belief that all problems have solutions. Different paths, different results, different meanings, but not always solutions.

The day has been good—and quiet. He hopes the days to come over the next few weeks will be the same, that they will allow Eagle Canyon to return to normal, at least as much as is possible after three people have been shot to death in church by one of their own.

§

Sitting in the police cruiser on surveillance, Esch has lots of time to review the tragedy, to consider its details and ramifications. She rotates her time between the homes of the three boys who survived the shooting. Chief Russo thinks it might be a sign of security for the boys and their families. Still, while it's important, it's also boring work, and she frets. To alleviate the boredom, she brings Eagle Canyon's police manual with her to study. The town's police force consists of six staff members: Chief Russo, Captain Green, Sergeant Collins, Esch and one other part-time officer, and Mrs. Collins, the dispatcher. Russo promised her when she came to work for the force that she would be considered for fulltime if one of his officers quit and moved on. Esch's training surpasses the other staff members, but she's young and inexperienced; she understands. She's built more like a librarian than a police officer.

Russo is comfortable with his two fulltime officers, but for the shooting he allows Esch to study the evidence due to her recent schooling. He complimented her on her composure at the church, telling her she handled the gore and chaos more professionally than his other officers. She initially studied forensics, but her pregnancy cut that short. On Monday afternoon she speaks with Pastor Chamberlain, Robbie's mother Carol Hollins, and two of the witnesses at the church. Official interviews, but away from the brown brick police building and the atmosphere of a murder investigation. As the only female officer, she presents a different face from the force, a gentler face, not the ticket writing, bar monitoring, vandalism investigation face that the town associates with the other officers. Esch's first assignment when she joined the force, the one for which she was hired, was as the liaison officer to the schools, especially for the elementary school and junior high. Speak with the students about vandalism, smoking, classroom behavior, respect for property, drug abuse, and underage drinking; all in a comfortable setting, away from parents. At the schools she doesn't tote her service revolver, since guns are not allowed in the building, but she does wear her uniform, cleaned and pressed. Esch feels at home with the kids, the part of the police motto about serving and being helpful that she most enjoys.

At Kevin's house Esch gets out of the patrol car and stands looking over the hood. She stretches and tries to remember the salient parts of her earlier interviews. Interviewing Carol Hollins, Esch saw where Robbie might have inherited his shyness. Sitting with Mrs. Hollins in her living room, a room Esch had been in years earlier, she spoke quietly and with introspection. Chief Russo's interview earlier in the day did not go well; Carol sobbed continuously, so he left and asked Esch to see if she could get anything. Esch sat on the sofa with Carol, was able to hug her, and listen more than interrogate. There was still crying, but it was controlled. She talked of Robbie's difficulties and of his gentility around her.

"Whenever he stepped outside the door, he became someone else. He never had a close friend. All through school he was isolated. Sometimes a good teacher would take him under her wing, and he'd have a better year, but when he got to junior high, there were separate classes for each subject and he just struggled. Everyone said the same thing, that he is such a nice boy, but so withdrawn. High school was more of the same. The counselor tried to put him in classes or activities where he might find a friend, but it never worked out."

Mrs. Hollins doesn't blame anyone but herself. Her sister will arrive mid-week so that she will have someone with her all the time, and she promised to visit Robbie every day. She also promised to be cooperative but can't say where he got the automatic rifle. After about an hour, she laid down with her head on Esch's lap and slept.

Esch's interview with Pastor Chamberlain took on a different tone. Esch had to hold her anger in, as she still felt that he should have come to the rescue of those in the room, to at least have run in the direction of the shots. "You told Chief Russo you were just outside the front of the church talking with some of the parishioners when you heard the shots. Where did you go then?"

"It was all so sudden. I'm not even sure I knew the sounds were gunshots. I don't think I've ever heard a shot fired in anger in my whole life. I was with Joe Malcolm; he had ushered the service for me. He immediately grabbed my arm and took me back inside the church and to the sacristy. I was there in no time. He pushed me inside and ordered me to lock the door from the inside. In there I prayed, but I can't really remember what I prayed for. It was Joe who came and got me later. I don't know how long I was in the sacristy, but when I came out, Joe took me to Mrs. Tuttle's room. I guess it was Joe and Gary Seymour who subdued Robbie."

"Where did your parishioners go?"

"I didn't know right away. I guess they went immediately to the police station. There was such confusion."

"Did you and Robbie have any problems?"

"Oh, no. He was happy here. He was even disappointed this spring when I told him he was too old to be a youth altar boy anymore, but that didn't last. He understood."

The answer didn't satisfy Esch, but she didn't want to pursue it any longer, and she felt no attachment to the reverend at the moment. From the church she drove to see Joe Malcolm, the hero of the tragedy. Russo was there asking all the questions, but Joe's presence impressed her. Joe was adamant that the shooting was not an act of God; tragedies such as these were devised by men here on earth, and that while prayer might ease some peoples' anxiety, answers would come from good police work. He verified Pastor Chamberlain's account, which relieved Esch at the time. Now, she recalls something else Chamberlain said to her. He said that in the sacristy, he examined his vestments for blood, thinking for sure he had been shot.

Esch knows who had blood on them. Kevin dic, and Marty, and Mrs. Tuttle, and Random, and Billy, and Bradley. Mrs. Tuttle wore a choir robe, while Billy and Bradley wore red acolyte robes with white covers. Not so white after all the shooting stopped. Esch turns around and looks to the hilltops above the Lutheran church on the north side of Eagle Canyon. Where were you? Why did you hide? Those people needed you.

CHAPTER 14

On Tuesday Russo drives to Denver to meet with the Denver Police Department about the shooting. They offer their expertise and crime labs, and Russo eagerly accepts. Esch sits with Robbie Hollins. A phone threat was made; an angry, impotent threat probably, but it has to be respected, so Robbie has a twenty-four-hour watch, and the cell room is locked from the inside. He will be transferred to a more secure facility soon, but the shooting is still considered a local crime to be handled by local law enforcement. Robbie's only exit from his cell was Monday afternoon when he was taken upstairs to the courthouse for his arraignment. The police station, municipal court, jail, and city hall all occupy the same building. In a town of fewer than two thousand citizens, it serves the purpose. It's an eight-to-five business on most days, closed on Sundays. An officer will answer the phone if anyone needs help. Robbie faces three counts of murder, three counts of attempted murder, and multiple lesser charges.

Chief Russo puts a port-a-pot and wash basin in Robbie's cell. He refused to leave his cell to use the toilet and soiled his mattress, so Russo brought the toilet to him, and it's working out. Under these conditions Russo is confident that Esch can monitor Robbie. Mrs. Collins knocks on the door. Esch admits Dr. Richards, a local psychiatrist, to speak with Robbie. Richards worked with Robbie briefly while he was a sophomore in high school, but found him simply to be withdrawn, an introvert, socially inept. Now, the doctor wants to re-examine his diagnosis, and the judge wants to see if Robbie will talk to the doctor.

"I can't leave you alone with him," Esch says. "He's under a twenty-four -hour watch."

"I understand," replies the doctor, "but a certain measure of confidentiality is necessary. Could you sit over by the door, and I'll sit close to Robbie, so that our conversation is private?"

"I can sit by the door, but Chief Russo ordered me not to allow you into the cell. You'll have to sit outside of his cell." Esch doesn't think Robbie will speak to the doctor, since he hasn't spoken with anyone else. His simple "No" to Chief Russo's question about whether or not his mother was a part of the killings has been his only audible sound. Esch rolls her chair to the far side of the room and sets up wooden chair next to the cell door. "Robbie, Doctor Richards is here to ask you some questions. I'll be by the door if you want something."

Doctor Richards sits and waits, saying nothing for over five minutes. Robbie lies on his cot with his body to the wall. Finally, the doctor speaks. "Robbie, I'd like to help you." The doctor's voice is quiet and respectful, like a veterinarian might speak to a cornered dog before he puts it to sleep. "We used to have a nice relationship, and I'd like to pick up there."

Despite the distance from the cell, Esch can hear the doctor. She senses guilt in his voice. Doctor Richards breaks the physical stereotype for a psychologist; tall and strong like a retired athlete, rugged features that resemble a rock climber, but today he slumps in the chair and wrings his hands. Esch took Burelle to see him once, but Burelle didn't return after that, and she wouldn't speak about her session. Robbie's silence makes her uncomfortable, but she doesn't turn away. She doesn't know what she's looking for, but she watches closely anyway. The squad car surveillance is boring, but her jail cell surveillance of Robbie Hollins has been fascinating, and she doesn't understand the difference.

"Robbie, I need your help here." Richards interlocks his fingers and drops his head onto the knuckle of the index finger. "I failed you, and . . . I'm sorry." He goes quiet for a moment, measuring his next words. "Before . . . when we were working together, I didn't think you were violent. It never crossed my mind. I focused in on your shyness and social withdrawal. When we talked, my focus was to help you overcome that, not to prevent something like this, because, like I said, I never anticipated you doing something like this." Richards lifts his head and rotates it from side to side. He knows he underestimated Robbie's abilities and that he didn't see the shame Robbie must have felt by being labeled mentally ill. He breathes out heavily. "I've gone through my notes looking for anything I might have missed, and I can't find anything. The pills I prescribed were for depression, to help you feel better about life. Are you still taking those?" The doctor knows that he miscalculated Robbie's depression and anxiety, and he believed Robbie would be able to cope better while medicated. "I shouldn't have left you alone just because your mother asked me to back off."

Esch wonders if Robbie is hearing anything Doctor Richards has said. She believes Robbie has checked out. He hasn't eaten and doesn't respond when Doctor Mason enters the cell twice each day to examine him. Chief Russo picked him up once and shook him, but Robbie's body went limp.

"Robbie, you have a choice here. You're going to be incarcerated for life, but under what conditions is still to be determined. I can help you. I don't believe a rational person walks into a church and murders three people for no reason; I just don't believe that." Dr. Richards pauses and looks back to Esch, as if for help. He turns back to the cell where a body lies curled up and motionless. "Come on, Robbie, help me help you, if not today, then soon. I'll be back on Friday, and we can talk again."

Esch, Richards, and Robbie Hollins occupy the room with bars, and each is confined, unable to reach another, and now the police deputy and the psychiatrist are as silent as the prisoner.

CHAPTER 15

Margaret Tuttle's funeral service is held on Wednesday morning at the Lutheran church where the shooting occurred. Reverend Chamberlain wears a reddish-purple chasuble and celebrates Holy Communion. The open casket reveals a slight smile, an optimistic visage. The eulogy, written by her husband and daughter, tells of Mrs. Tuttle's life as a teacher and a server to others. Her good works were an indication of her salvation, and the congregation is confident she now resides with the Father in Heaven. She was a Christian and she believed.

The funeral for the two slain acolytes, William Dunn and Bradley Arnold, takes place the next morning, but is much more difficult for the town. Again, Reverend Chamberlain officiates, but in his grief, he breaks down during the service, causing the congregation to openly weep. He wears a white vestment. The boys' caskets rest side-by-side, closed, and laden with flowers. Billy is the oldest of four children, while Bradley is an only child. Was and was. The boys' eulogies focus on their activities as teenagers and their close friendship. Bradley's father, the owner of the town's tire store, stands dignified in front of the congregation wearing his only suit, all three buttons fastened. He recalls the hunting and camping trips that he, Billy's father, Billy, and Bradley made each fall. In preparation for giving his son's eulogy, he spent an hour with a scrub brush trying to get the oil and grit out from under his fingernails.

"Fathers and sons. The best moments of our lives. The four of us eagerly looked forward to our fall trip each year." Mr. Arnold pauses, not to collect himself, but to privately picture the forest scene around the tents. He smiles and continues. "Last year, Brad got his first buck and Billy got his second. That first one is always the best one." Mr. Arnold won't have a second son to teach the ritual to, but he isn't thinking about that now as he details the hunting trip. "My boy will be fourteen-years-old forever. He'll be the funny kid with the irrepressible cowlick who never tired of playing practical jokes on his mother. He loved his grandparents, and they will miss him as much as Heather and I will." Mr. Arnold stops and nods to two sets of grandparents in the front pew. "Neighbors, we had a terrible thing happen to our community, and it's imperative we find out why this tragedy was visited on us. What got into that boy's head? What happened to his heart that sent him into this sacred place to do such harm? Did anyone see it coming? I want to know why my boy was killed. What do we need to change to see that this doesn't happen to other communities? I want Eagle Canyon to be a lesson, not just an incident. I'm not smart enough to know the answers to my questions, but I hope those who are will study this and see what can be done about it in the future." He gathers his notes and starts to move away from the pulpit but stops. "One more thing. Let's not hate that boy who's sitting over in our jail. He's our link to understanding what happened, and there needs to be a purpose to his life. God knows, his mother will need our support too."

Billy Dunn's eulogy is read by his younger brother who is accompanied by the entire family to the altar. The twelve-year-old boy makes no plea to forgive Robbie or to support Mrs. Hollins. While he reads, Billy's mother stands stoically, her jaw clenched, her eyes glazed.

The procession to the cemetery stretches over two miles. At the gravesites Reverend Chamberlain beseeches the Lord for understanding in the days ahead. "God gives us the choice. We can choose violence, or we can choose gentility." And again, he asks for prayers for the boys and their families. Hogan Tree, Morvid Tree, Random Tree, and Burelle Oakley attend both services. As the town disperses, Random tugs on his mother's hand to stay longer at the gravesite.

"What is it Random?" asks Burelle.

"Billy's dad is my baseball coach. He looks sad and I just want to watch him for a minute."

Burelle kneels in front of her son and then sits in the grass. She is unconcerned about soiling her black dress. "What is it, honey?"

"What if it had been me? Where would I be now?" Random hasn't taken his stare off Billy Dunn's father, but he finally turns into his mother's eyes and begins to cry uncontrollably. The little boy who cradled his dying teacher in his lap, who stood before the reporters to answer their incomprehensible questions, who has pretended to be strong for his mother, now cries openly for the first time.

Burelle hugs him into her bosom, and Random melts into his mother like butter into warm mashed potatoes. She rocks him gently. She knows she could have lost him last Sunday, but for some inexplicable reason, his life was spared. Every moment since then, she has known that Random Tree could have been Billy Dunn or Bradley Arnold, and she has been terrified.

Neither Burelle nor Random notice that Hogan has remained, standing behind them, watching over them.

CHAPTER 16

Robbie Hollins hangs himself with his bed sheet on Thursday evening before answering any questions, before he explains to anyone why he carried a rifle into church. Many of the townsfolk feel cheated. They are angry at Robbie, but also at Chief Russo for allowing it to happen. Shouldn't he have had a deputy watching Robbie every minute? When Burelle explains to Random that he doesn't have to be afraid anymore of Robbie, Random tells her he never was. He had seen something in Robbie's eyes. Something passed between them, and Robbie lowered his rifle and left the room.

§

Suicide with collateral damage. What a waste. Chief Russo stares at Robbie's naked body as the coroner examines it in the cell, a body not much more lifeless than it had been for the four previous nights. Russo hasn't investigated a murder in Eagle Canyon before, although murders were common on his last job in Chicago. Common? There's nothing common about any murder. How do I proceed now without Robbie, he asks himself? Is this over now, except for the grieving and paperwork?

Robbie wasn't a violent kid, but he obtained a powerful weapon and committed an unspeakable crime. His mom knew of his struggles, the school knew, he was seeing a psychiatrist, but nobody tells me. Robbie's mental, but it's kept a secret. The stigma of seeing a shrink. I don't know what I could have done had I been warned, but if I'd have known, then, maybe I could have foreseen this. Russo turns slowly as the body is placed on the gurney. The chief drops his chin onto his chest and shakes his head ever so slightly. I wish I had been harder on Robbie when I first interviewed him. I wish I had forced a confession out of him. The court ordered me to go easy, but now I'll never know for certain.

Reverend Chamberlain told me that Robbie was a strange boy, and now he is in "God's kingdom." What kind of a response is that? God had nothing to do with this! The chief walks into the now vacant cell, turns and looks outward. Russo's on the inside row. No, it's not over. Pray all you want for comfort and solace or healing or the souls, but don't ask God to tell you why. A boy with a gun did this, a boy from a fairly normal family, and if answers are forthcoming, I will be the one to give them.

§

Fulton Tree finally returns home from his extended stay at the cabin on Thursday night. He showers and shaves and then goes to Burelle's section of Morvid's house, entering without knocking, using his key. Random looks up from the kitchen table where he is finishing his supper and says hi. Fulton lifts him up and looks him all over in a mock search for wounds. "I see you survived. No bullet holes, huh?" says Fulton.

"No. Where have you been?"

"Working. Someone has to pay the bills." Fulton sets his son down and asks where Burelle is. Fulton never refers to Burelle as Random's mother in his presence.

"Back there," says Random pointing to the bedroom. "Mom! Dad's here!"

"Come on out, Burelle. I ain't drunk. I just want to talk to you about the shooting."

Burelle opens her door but stays framed in the jamb. Three years earlier, Hogan rebuilt the front wall and door, made it stronger with layered two-by-sixes, and installed a deadbolt lock; in effect trying to construct a safe room for Burelle and Random. It hasn't worked as planned. Fulton removed the lock and installed one of his own. After that, Hogan suggested that Burelle and Random come live with him, but Fulton warned her that if she did, he'd hurt her and hurt Random. She never told Hogan of Fulton's threat; she just declined his offer. A tenuous truce remains. Burelle and Random live in Morvid's house, but Hogan's unspoken threat to his son keeps Fulton from hitting Burelle anymore. Burelle talks to no one about her situation. She accepts it and lives each day.

"Morvid said you were staying at the cabin, doing some fence work along the property line. Did you hear about Robbie?" asks Burelle.

"The work was over the hill on Paul Jackson's. He has all that land that gets trespassed on by the tourists, and he wants it fenced off to keep the horses in. Yeah, I heard about Robbie. Fucking coward! He gets to go out on his own terms. Russo should have shot him at the church and then dragged his body down to the park so the whole town could see. I know where he could of hung. Nobody in this town has any guts. None of them deserve any better than this shitty little town offers them." Fulton turns to Random. "You think that would have been fair for what he did, boy?"

Random doesn't speak; he just stares. He never understands why his father comes over at all just to be mean to his mother.

Fulton opens the refrigerator and lifts out the pitcher of tea. He takes a glass from the cabinet and sits at the table. After filling the glass, he taps his palm on the opposite side of the table, a sign for Burelle to sit down. She obeys but watches her son and not his father. Fulton stares out the window over the sink and sips his tea. Random hasn't moved since Fulton came in, but now he wanders over to a two-seater couch, sits down, and opens one of his books. He understands that he is not part of the conversation any longer, and he is trained not to interrupt his dad.

"How come you weren't in church protecting my boy when Robbie started shooting?"

"I was there at church; I just wasn't in the Sunday school classroom." Burelle doesn't need Fulton's accusations to feel guiltier.

"No excuse. You should've known." Fulton turns to glare at Burelle. "He had a rifle, for Christ's sake! How could you not have known?"

"Esch said that Robbie went out to his car after the service to get his gun and then returned through the back door. Nobody saw him or could have known. They're still trying to figure it out."

"You're pretty calm about all this, Burelle. Random could've been killed." Fulton speaks quietly, in measured tones. "Then what would you have done? Without Random, you'd have nowhere to live, because I'd kick you out of here." Fulton winks at Burelle and turns back to the window. Burelle waits, not responding with any of the things she wants to say. She looks over to Random and feels ashamed. Random keeps his head down, pretending to read.

Fulton rotates his head slowly back to Burelle. "I'll tell you what, Burelle. I'll let it go this time, but don't you ever put my boy in danger again." He stares at her in silence before getting up and leaving. At the door he turns back to Random. "School's starting pretty soon, isn't it? What grade will you be in this year?"

"Third."

§

Well past midnight Chief Russo sits alone in front of Robbie's cell. A deputy sits at the front desk manning the phone, but the crowd of officials who were in the jail hours earlier has left. Russo's tired; tired from today, tired from the events of five days of death. Still, his mind hasn't been affected. The cot is stripped of its sheets, and the cell has been scrubbed. Russo hired a cleaning service, a married couple from Denver to come up and do it. "So, this is what it was all about, huh, Robbie? You could have done this and not killed Brad and Billy, you know," he says aloud as if Robbie is still curled up on the cot. The chief goes silent. He slumps in the chair, rolls his head back, and puts his stout hand up to his chin while resting his elbow on his chest.

"Telephone, boss."

"Who is it?"

"Carol Hollins. She's crying."

Chief Russo gets up from the chair with a grunt, walks to the main office, and takes the phone from the hand of the officer. Before he answers, he sits at the desk. He motions to the officer to get him a cup of coffee, his tenth of the day. "Hi, Carol. Are you at home?" Russo nods his head in appreciation to the officer when his coffee is set on the desk. The chief drinks it black and strong, stronger than anyone else in the department likes. He listens, but he has no answers. The man whose job it is to protect this town has as many questions as anyone. When he responds to Robbie's mother's comments, it's in a soft, fatherly voice. Eventually, Carol Hollins falls asleep before hanging up. Russo listens to the silence, giving her time to wake up, but after a few minutes, he knows she won't. She will be haunted by her son's actions for the rest of her life; unable to explain where she went wrong, blaming herself. Russo disconnects by placing the receiver in the cradle quietly. He'll talk with Carol periodically, but he doubts he'll ever see her at the range again.

§

Burelle can't sleep. Robbie Hollins pointed a deadly rifle at her son five days earlier, and yet she somehow feels sad about his death. Robbie's picture from the Eagle Canyon Tribune when he was being taken out of the church last Sunday is the only image she has to hang on to. She sits in her nightgown at her two-person kitchen table studying Robbie's face. His head seems to lurch forward as the police officers escort him to an awaiting patrol car. His eyes must have caught the photographer just as the photo was being snapped because he seems to be staring into Burelle's eyes. Those eyes aren't defiant nor are they threatening. To Burelle, those eyes seem to be searching for someone, maybe his mother. Desperate. Were these the eyes that stared into Random's eyes? Burelle slides the photo off to the side, but Robbie's eyes remain focused on hers. She has nothing to compare those eyes to, except maybe her own in the mirror.

Burelle is drawn to people's eyes. Some people observe faces and see wrinkles or dimples. She looks into the eyes and can travel into a person's past. People look at Morvid and are charmed by his smile, the old banker who laughs frequently, who has been a fixture in Eagle Canyon for as long as anyone can remember. Burelle sees his past and wonders when the fungus began to eat away at his soul. Her heart pounds. When Random was born, she had hope. Her mother promised to stop drinking and help out; she told Burelle to finish high school, and she would watch Random. But her mother left and Burelle had to quit school. Fulton ridiculed her to his friends. Then he joined the Army, and things were better again. She worked part time jobs. Living with Morvid was lonely, but she promised herself to do whatever was necessary to keep Random safe and get out of town before Fulton returned. Morvid was fools' gold. She should have seen it that night he described his proficiency with a pistol after Random had gone to bed, but she didn't. She didn't grasp the old man's meaning. It has always been a battle with Fulton and Morvid, a conflict she is destined to lose personally, but she has kept Random secure, at least that's what she tells herself. But the Sunday killings whisper something different.

I should have taken Esch's advice and bought a gun. I should have gotten on the bus and fled, but I had nowhere to go. I should have found my mom. I had three years without Fulton and should have left. But I didn't. Burelle won't forgive herself.

§

Burelle hasn't worked all week, and Random doesn't let his mother out of his sight. He's always been affectionate, but this week he's clingy. Hogan notices it too. They've had dinner twice, but Random wasn't hungry. He hasn't eaten much, complaining of a stomachache. Hogan reassures Burelle that these afflictions will be temporary. Still, she worries about him when she will have to return to working. Mrs. Berthoud tells Burelle that Random is welcome to come with her to the diner while she works. "School starts soon and until then I'll put him to work busing tables," she said only partly joking. Esch volunteered her parents as babysitters too. Burelle accepted both offers, even though the dark circles around Random's eyes tell her to keep him close.

CHAPTER 17

Morvid and the journalism student sip coffee at the Hiway 6 where they have agreed to meet to conclude the final chapters of Morvid's story. What began in late July as three or four sessions to meet the requirements of a single assignment has expanded into a longer paper, one that may fulfill the requirements of his senior thesis. The student met Burelle, Random, and Fulton after the shooting, and he is uncomfortable meeting at the house any longer. Fulton especially makes him feel uneasy. Morvid doesn't care where they meet; he just wants to talk, to tell his story. It's September and summer is ending. Morvid has come to believe that each summer will be his last, that his life is aligned with the seasons. He tells this to anyone who will listen, and he has for the last three years, each year getting more critical. Fourscore-years-old seems to be the cut-off date for a good, productive life.

"Gertie left Hogan around '65, I believe, about a dozen years ago. Fulton was about twelve or thirteen. I retired from the bank a few years earlier and was comfortable. Neither Hogan nor Fulton said much. One day she's here, the next day she's not. I guess they just fell out of love, or the American lifestyle was just too much for her. She went back to New Zealand. Hogan never talked about it; he just worked harder. Fulton seemed happy about it; he got more freedom. Gertie was always trying to teach him manners and such, but he was headstrong and wanted to be a boy. That's when Hogan really started to withdraw, but it could have been his increasing trouble with hearing. Fulton was a big boy, probably taller than his dad by then. Those two would go at it, that's for sure.

"All of my wife's kids had moved away, and the last of my two were married and gone to Phoenix and Dallas, so the house was empty. Sometime after that, I suggested to Hogan that he sell his place and move in, but he declined. Fulton liked the idea and began to spend more time here. He took up in one of the upstairs bedrooms and made it his own. I couldn't understand how Hogan could just let his own son move and leave the responsibility of raising him to an old man. Anyway, in high school he was the best athlete in Eagle Canyon. He was the quarterback in football and led the conference in scoring in basketball. People would come up and talk to me about him all the time. He had his pick of the girls too. I still like to brag on him, as you can tell. He had a football game his senior year when we were playing one of them suburban schools that was ranked number one, and they just could not contain him. Their coach tried everything to stop him, even trying to hurt him after the plays in the pileups. In the fourth quarter, we were down by a touchdown, and Fulton just willed his teammates down the field for the final score. He ran it in from about six yards, and then he rolled out and ran over two of their guys to get the two-point conversion. Our fans went wild. We had a good chance to win the championship, but the coach benched Fulton for drinking, and we lost the last two games. The same happened his junior year. The coach cost Fulton a scholarship. That's why he never went to college.

"Instead, he joined the Army and went to Vietnam. That's where he grew up and became more responsible. He got there just as Nixon was Vietnamizing the whole thing. I like to tell people that the war ended when the gooks found out that my grandson had showed up. It didn't, of course, but it was ending. Fulton was an infantry soldier like I was in The Great War. He sent me back a string of ears from his kills, some big ones and some little ones. He said Charlie came in all shapes and sizes. We didn't do that in my war, but I guess the rules changed for today's soldiers. Fighting up close, I understood, but when he returned home, he got into a big row with his dad. Hogan said cutting up the enemy wasn't right, but then Hogan was on a ship. He fired shells from miles away and didn't see much real blood. I'd have thought that Hogan would be happy to see his son come home safe, but he didn't seem to. They hadn't gotten along so good before he left, and it didn't improve any when Fulton returned.

"He was always an edgy kid, but when he came back, he had some anger in him. None of our soldiers from that war got any respect when they returned. Wasn't fair. I left out a part about Fulton. He got Burelle pregnant in high school; she wasn't really his girlfriend, but you know how those things happen. That woman police officer you met was his girl back then, but this is a small town. Anyway, Random was born after Fulton's junior year. He never married Burelle, but he never told anybody that Random wasn't his kid. While Fulton was off in Vietnam, Burelle's mother ran off with a fellow from the South, so I had her and Random move in here. We sold her trailer house, and I put the money in an account for her at the bank. It wasn't much, but it was something. I liked having them in the house; it had gotten so lonely. They needed someone too. Burelle grew up poor and her mother was, well, kind of a bar woman. Those years with Random were really fun, and I think Burelle was happy with the arrangement. We were never close, but she trusted me to take care of Random sometimes when she worked.

"Fulton seemed okay with it when he came back from Vietnam, but he didn't want Burelle to tie him down, so we moved her into that outside set of rooms. That way, he could see his boy, but not be married. There were times when he went over to see Random, but his anger took over, and I had to break 'em up. He never hit his boy, though. Random's the next generation Tree, so he has to live here. Four generations right now live in Eagle Canyon, and like all families we have our squabbles, but we're doing pretty good."

The student interrupts Morvid. "So, except for Hogan and his son and grandson, the rest of the Trees left Eagle Canyon?"

"Yes. You know how kids are. They need to set off on their own and establish their own families. Eagle Canyon is my place, Hogan's place. I suspect that it will always be Fulton's place too. He'll settle down and get married and continue to live in this house along with the family he creates long after I've left this earth."

The student accepts that and brings Morvid back to the tragic recent event.

"The killings were an aberration for Eagle Canyon, and things will get back to normal pretty soon, and we'll be able to focus on the things that matter. You know. Family, jobs, and the like. The shooting at the church just has us re-examining things that don't need to be brought up. We need to move on and forget about what happened. We'll take care of our own, understand, but we need to put it behind us and get on with our lives. It just happened out of the blue, and we couldn't predict it, so why dwell on it. We need to forget about it. Say a prayer for them boys that died and let them be in peace."

The journalism student has not asked many questions, but this last comment raises one. "Mr. Tree, what about the families of the people who were murdered or those who witnessed it happen? Are they supposed to just forget and move on also?"

"No, those families won't forget, but they all have to move forward. Nothing they can do now about it but move ahead."

CHAPTER 18

The journalism student knocks on Hogan's door hoping Hogan will comment on some of his father's statements, but Hogan declines. Unlike his father, who will tell the most intimate family stories to complete strangers, Hogan keeps his life concealed. He reveals his story only to his dog. He knows Tinker doesn't understand and can't respond, but Tinker is Hogan's sounding board. She sits patiently and listens, whether it is in the house or on the back porch or walking along the river. Hogan has two voices: one for work and public conversation, and one for contemplation and recovery. If Tinker was human, she would remember more, much more, but as his best friend, she does understand his moods and wags her tail or nuzzles his leg accordingly. She also has a good feel for those who visit her master. She isn't a barker; Tinker leaves the room or goes to the corner when disagreeable people are around. In that way she mimics Hogan. While the journalism student briefly talks with Hogan, Tinker steps onto the porch, listens to the two men's voices, and lies down nearby.

§

Hogan checked himself into the West Denver Institute in '61. He and Gertie discussed it at length; she had seen his fall coming but was powerless to help him. His introspective nature was what had first attracted her to him back in Australia, back in '43 when he had been hospitalized with a hip wound after a Japanese plane attacked his ship. Several of his fellows were killed, and the destroyer had sunk. Gertie served as a nurse's aide; it seemed as though everyone in Australia and New Zealand worked to help the war effort.

She and Hogan talked about the war and about war in general. Hogan saw beyond this war. It was the first time Gertie ever had, and she fell in love with this American who cried for his fellows and worried about a man's purpose.

Hogan recovered and went back to the war. He wrote to Gertie nearly every day, letters that were delivered to her in bunches, so she received chapters of his thoughts rather than snippets. Somewhere on the drive to the Philippines, he contracted malaria and was sent back to Darwin, and they married. At the time, her family was alarmed that their teenage daughter would marry an American, especially one who wasn't a farmer. Hogan had to return to the States without her when the war ended, but he came back to her— to New Zealand in late '45, where they stayed with her family for five years. Gertie's family dropped their alarm and accepted the gentle man, the quiet man, the American who loved Gertie completely. He became a farmer during those years, an extremely hard worker on the ranch where Gertie's family lived on the north island near Rotorua.

§

Chief Russo visits Hogan twice during the week to talk about Random, to see if Hogan's grandson is handling the stress. Tinker sits with the two men as they talk, allowing each man to scratch her shoulders occasionally. After each visit, Hogan takes Tinker on walks and speaks quietly to her. Upon returning home, Tinker naps and Hogan reads, or at least holds a book.

Hogan thinks about Chief Russo. Hogan admires him. The police chief is a problem-solver, a man you can trust with a secret, a man who will try to do the right thing, even if it means bending a few rules and regulations along the way. They attended high school together, although Russo is a couple of years younger than Hogan. Gertie liked him on the few occasions when the two couples got together in the '60s after Russo returned from Chicago to take over Eagle Canyon's police force. Unlike him, Russo is a religious man and has a hearty laugh. Do those things go together? Until Gertie left and he withdrew, Hogan liked to talk philosophy with Russo.

Each had a perspective. Gertie would say, after Russo and his wife had gone home, that she loved the conversations between a religious man and a philosophical man. She would laugh at how Russo would always lean forward, lean into the person he was most interested in seeing his point, sometimes even placing his big hand on a knee or shoulder, and say, "Now listen, if you consider this from all sides," meaning his side. Russo's way drew people close, but Gertie would laugh that Hogan leaned away.

Tinker stands, arches her back, makes a quick circle, and then slumps back into the same space. Hogan scratches her neck. After dinner on the last night before Gertie left, they had sat with Russo and his wife. Hogan didn't tell him; he just didn't know how. Fulton was at the babysitter's house along with Russo's boys. Hogan talked all around it, but couldn't bring himself to say, "Gertie's leaving and going home to New Zealand. Fulton's just wearing her out." Instead, the conversation was philosophic. Was the universe created with a purpose, or was God just experimenting? Is God done or is he still creating? After all, said Russo, there seems to be so much empty space out there and lots of time to keep building new planets or solar systems. He was provocative in his kidding. A dozen years ago. On that last night, Gertie asked Russo if a person had to believe to go to Heaven, and the chief answered after a moment of thought that he didn't think so. "God won't ask you if you believed. After all, by then you'll be standing in front of Him at the Pearly Gates, so it will be pretty obvious. God'll just want to know if you tried." Hogan liked that. A lot. Did you try? Sounds like a question God would ask. Like Russo, God will lean into your space, maybe place His hand on your shoulder, and ask, "Did you try?"

§

Random calls later in the afternoon to see if Grampa wants to take him to dinner. Burelle suggests the new McDonald's. Hogan vetoes that in favor of the old hamburger joint downtown, the one that will be replaced eventually by McDonald's. Besides, Randy would need to scrape off all the fixins that are put on his hamburger at McDonald's; at The Spud he can get his burger and fries and add all the catsup he wants. No onions or pickles or lettuce. Hogan will meet them outside Morvid's fence at five for the short walk to town. Hogan hangs up the phone and goes to the refrigerator for his bottle of salad dressing that he will take to dinner to pour on his burger. Hogan empties the last of the bag of dog food into Tinker's metal dish, brushes her a few times while she eats, and then takes a shower. He has lived in this house for over twenty-five years. He's kept it up, painted, clean, and comfortable. But he wouldn't miss it if he ever left; it has never been home.

CHAPTER 19

The janitorial position at the police department opens at the end of August, and Russo, in spite of all the activity from the shooting, hires Burelle. Esch has been lobbying to secure this job for Burelle for several months. It pays only slightly above the minimum wage, but the job provides security, security in the sense that if Burelle is part of the department, the police will consider her as family. It's a day job with regular hours, and she will begin the day after Labor Day, the first day of school. While Random attends school, Burelle will clean the station, and there is some overtime, certainly better than house cleaning or being a waitress at the various cafes around Eagle Canyon. The previous janitor retired after nearly three decades on the job, so Burelle believes she can finally make plans for the future. Chief Russo also tells Burelle that the dispatcher job will open up in a year or so, the promise of a promotion if she works hard until then.

Random and Burelle surprise Hogan at school, bringing sandwiches and the news. Burelle's excitement is transferred to Random, who runs around the small cafeteria while his mother and grandfather talk.

"It's time, Burelle," says Hogan. "I've fixed that small space for Random's bedroom."

§

Hogan informs Morvid later in the afternoon that Burelle and Random will be leaving and moving in with him immediately. "Fulton might say that Random can't go, but you tell him that I said not to interfere."

"I'll tell him," says Morvid, "but I can't guarantee anything."

§

Fulton throws all of Burelle's dresses and blouses that are hanging in her closet to the floor and then repeats his action with her underclothes from the bureau. It isn't an extensive wardrobe, much of it left by her mother when she left Eagle Canyon, when she left Burelle. He walks on the pile, then stands and urinates on the clothes. He doesn't know who he's angry at, but he usually takes it out on Burelle. In the kitchen Fulton empties the refrigerator onto the floor and hurls a flower vase against the wall. "Something to think about when you come home from your fancy new job, Burelle. Something to chew on, bitch. Remember this when you're at Hogan's house," he says aloud. Fulton leaves to join his buddies on a Labor Day bird hunting trip in western Kansas.

§

On Saturday Hogan and Esch help Burelle and Random move their few possessions. She can't afford to replace her soiled wardrobe, so Esch takes it to a laundromat and double washes all of Burelle's and Random's clothes. Hogan gives Esch money for her to buy a few school shirts for Random and two work uniforms for Burelle. Morvid stands on the sidewalk and watches as they vacate his house, but there is nothing for him to do. "You make sure Random comes around, so I can see him." When everything is removed, Burelle gives Morvid a cursory hug. He smells like Fulton, of beer and cigarettes, just like her mother smelled. A dozen thoughts pass through her mind as she watches Random say goodbye. Burelle is good at standing off to the side and watching. Over five years in the big house, mostly colored by the last three when Fulton returned from the Army. Morvid helped her get her G.E.D. during those first years, tutoring her in math and science, sitting with her at the dining room table. He had a plan. Fulton would be a changed man when he came home, and maybe he would marry Burelle. He wanted her to be ready for him, and she couldn't tell Morvid no. No, he won't want me. No, he is abusive. No, he raped me. That first day home from the war, Fulton ordered Burelle out, and Morvid just stood by. She sees Fulton in his Army uniform, ordering Morvid. "She isn't staying here with us, old man." Somehow, Morvid had known because the guest quarters were ready for her and Random. Twin beds in the one room, a clean bathroom with towels, a stocked kitchen. Morvid didn't challenge Fulton. Fulton left to celebrate his homecoming, and Morvid helped her and his great-grandson move out of the big house.

Random shakes his great grandfather's hand and says, "Bye, Morvid."

Burelle steps back to Morvid and hugs him again. "Thank you for the room, and . . . I know you hoped for something different."

§

At Hogan's house Random finally has his own bedroom, even if it is a redesigned storage space at the top of the stairs. He calls it his pirate cove, since it has a secret cubby hole next this bed.

Hogan takes Burelle into his bedroom and shows her where he keeps his pistol, a Colt .357 revolver. "It's always loaded, and it's easy to use." The three rooms are located next to one another on the second floor.

Burelle shakes her head. "I don't know if I could, Hogan," she says while taking hold of it.

"I hope you never have to see, and I'm pretty sure he won't come here. He knows I will, but just in case." Hogan demonstrates how to open the drawer where it is stowed. "I installed a simple lock so Random can't get at it, but it's still quickly accessible."

Esch returns in the afternoon with the clothes and lunch. She is upbeat, especially with Random. She slips an eye-patch over his head to compliment his sword and calls him Long John Silver. "Aye, matey, do you have your ship all set up?" Random assures her that he does. He takes Esch by the hand upstairs to show her his cove, leaving his mother and grandfather at the kitchen table.

"We each have our own journey in life, but it helps to sometimes stop off at an inn along the way to rest and share, Burelle. You've had a tough life, but we're gonna make it easier for now, for both you and Randy."

"Esch and I always swam in the trouble pool as kids, but I think I was in the deep end more than her. Random changed me. Overnight. I made promises, and I've kept most of them. Being here, it already is easier. I can't tell you how good this feels." Burelle leans over and lays her head on Hogan's shoulder.

Hogan wants to apologize, but he stays silent. It should have been three years ago.

§

Random's first full day at school is Tuesday, the day after Labor Day. His classmates avoid asking questions about the shooting. Marty and Kevin are both in his class, and the school counselor sits in on the first day. Tara, the younger sister of Billy Dunn, does not attend, but her family has made plans for her to start a week late, to allow for classes to begin as normally as possible, and if she is ready. As the school liaison officer, Esch visits each class at the elementary school during the first day. Her message is the same. "A terrible thing occurred in church this summer, but Eagle Canyon is on the mend. Random, Kevin, and Marty were all brave boys, and we should be proud of them, but don't ask them to tell you about it. They've been asked too many times to tell their stories, so if you have questions, please ask me or your teacher."

§

On Wednesday morning Fulton storms into the school demanding to know which classroom is Random's. The startled secretary recognizes him. "Mrs. Clark's room, 27, half-way down the hall on the left." She realizes immediately her mistake and goes into the principal's office to tell Mr. Springston. He first calls Hogan in his office, but doesn't get an answer, then hurries down the hall to diffuse the situation. He is a beat behind. Fulton has marched to Random's room and pulled his son out of class. Once outside and into his truck, Fulton isn't sure what to do, so he drives to the police station and takes Random inside. The school calls the police to inform both Chief Russo and Burelle, who has given the police number as the place where she can be reached in an emergency. Chief Russo is just exiting the front door of the station for his cruiser when Fulton drives up.

"Mornin', Fulton. How about you leave your boy with Mrs. Collins and come have a seat in my office. You can tell me about your huntin' trip, and I'll get one of my men to drive Random back to school."

Fulton nods and looks down at Random. "You go on. Me and the chief will talk." Fulton turns back to Chief Russo and follows him into his office. From behind a smoky window across from the chief's office, Burelle watches. She was told by Russo not to attend to her son, to allow the officers to take him back to school, to avoid a clash with Fulton in this place. As the patrol car pulls out of the parking lot, Hogan flags it down. He has run from the school to the station.

"It's okay, Mr. Tree," says the officer. "Fulton is with Chief Russo. He'll talk him down and set him right. Random here is okay. Why don't you jump in the back and ride back to school with us?"

Hogan is visibly shaken, but he doesn't want to transfer his anger onto Random. "You okay," he asks. Random nods. Hogan reaches in and rubs the back of his hand over Random's cheek. "You go on back to school and forget about this. I'll talk to your dad and the chief to see what happened, and we'll talk it over tonight at dinner."

The cruiser drives off, and Hogan watches. What he wants to do and what he can do at the moment are two different things, but he knows this can't be ignored. He turns toward the station and stares, contemplating the immediate and the not so distant. He trusts Russo, so he turns again and heads back toward Whitman Elementary. The walk will settle him some and give him time to think.

After Chief Russo allows Fulton talk about his hunting trip, and after Fulton has relaxed somewhat, Russo asks, "What were you planning to do with your boy just now?"

"I don't know, maybe take him home and mess around with him some. I don't get to see him much." Fulton keeps his head up and smiles as he talks.

Russo slides up in his chair in a subtle move to challenge Fulton. "Son, what you did by taking Random out of school like that comes pretty close to breaking several laws, and I'm not going to allow you to behave like that again. I know about how things have been tough for you this past year, what with the mine closing and jobs being scarce. I know that Burelle and Random moved out." The chief pauses. "But none of that excuses your actions this morning. I've excused your recent behavior, but no more. You're an adult and you need to get control of yourself. You need to stop drinking so much and get a permanent job, quit blaming others for your misfortunes." Fulton looks down, and Russo wants to reach over and lift Fulton's face, forcing him to look into the chief's eyes.

Finally, Fulton raises his head. "I know. Sometimes I just can't seem to control my anger."

"That's enough of that, son. That's not how an adult behaves. When you get the next wild-ass hair up your butt, you call me. Whatever I'm doing, I'll drop it and see you. We've got to get this irrational behavior under control. Do you hear?"

When Fulton leaves, Chief Russo finds Burelle. "Are you alright?"

"Yes, sir. I've sort of been expecting something to happen since I moved out." Burelle bends down to fasten the electric cord to the vacuum cleaner.

"Burelle, let that go and look at me." Russo steps forward and takes her forearm, not like he would when escorting a prisoner, but more in an attempt to show concern. "Let's go into my office and talk."

In his office Russo guides Burelle to a chair. He walks to the coffee machine and pours two cups, and then pulls his chair around the big, cluttered desk so that he is sitting next to her without any barrier in between. "It's been a rough few weeks, hasn't it?" He waits, but Burelle doesn't speak. "Esch told me about your move. Told me Fulton was pretty mad about it. Do you want to tell me anything about it?"

Burelle curls her tongue behind her lower front teeth and wonders what good it will do, but she has to admit to herself that it feels good for someone to ask. Esch knows and Hogan knows, but with them it is mostly an unspoken contract. "Camping." She looks up and breathes deeply. She inspects the fat, reddish face of Chief Russo and finds it comforting. She rubs her hands over her thighs and breathes heavily again. "Fulton is a dangerous man, and I'm afraid of him."

Russo waits, giving Burelle time, giving himself time. We understand so little, he thinks. "Go on, Burelle."

"My life up to now hasn't been so good. I know people look down on me, Mr. Russo, but they don't know. Once, I had a chance, back in high school, but everything changed because I got pregnant. Since the birth of Random, I've sort of been dependent on the Trees. My mom left, you remember, and I just couldn't make it on my own, even though I did have the trailer. When Morvid asked me to move in with him, I did, and for a few years it was okay. But then Fulton came back and wanted," Burelle pauses. Her jaw quivers and, to Russo, she looks defeated, but she finds a word. "Rights. And I had nothing to bargain with except Random. So I stayed. It's nice to be out of there."

§

"What did you think when your dad showed up in class this morning, Randy?" asks Hogan between bites of his hamburger. Burelle lays her fork on her plate and waits for her son's response.

"Nothing much. He was just acting like he does sometimes."

"What did your friends think?"

"They mostly thought he was there to show off. He was smiling and said hi to Mrs. Clark and said we were going fishing. So, I just went with him."

"But you're all right now?" asks Hogan.

"Yeah. It was no big deal. That's just the way he is."

Burelle watches her son finish his dinner. How can an eight-year-old have such an attitude? Danger swirls around him, and yet he dodges it instinctively. Do I worry unnecessarily? She glances at Hogan. He rushed to the police station to help, maybe I can relax a bit and start planning a future, thinks Burelle.

"Finish, Mom, so I can leave the table."

CHAPTER 20

On the journalism student's last session with Morvid, he asks if there are any aspects of his life in America that he wants to add to his story.

"I'm eighty, as I think I already told you, and I know I've confused you some in my story. Your professor suggested me because of that story the Denver Post did on me a few years back. People keep looking into my past and seeing something. I sure wish they'd look into my future and tell me where it's heading. I'm sure you read it. That story used me as an example of all of us American families with multiple generations of wartime experiences. Fulton was having a hard time finding a job, and they wanted to make it seem as though it was because of Vietnam. Maybe it was, but I never had a difficult time going back to work when I came home from France. Different time, I guess.

"What I think is that men from war have an anger, and it takes a little time to get rid of it. You have to be patient and give them that time. It'll pass. The country owes us that time for what we did. When I came home, I wanted my wife to call me by my French name. That sounds silly, I know, but I liked how Jaures Tree sounded. I never told my wife where it came from; I made up a story about how I stole it from a French socialist who had been assassinated before the war for trying to keep France from going to war. Noble. Danver said my name was Morvid and that was that. But I bought my tombstone and had it etched Morvid Jaures Tree. It just proves that a man can be several men over the course of his lifetime and still come out at the end.

"That shooting at the church was terrible, and my family was right in the middle of it. It makes no sense to most people; they keep saying, 'Why did it happen here?' Hell, we don't know, but it did. My great grandson was in the room and got blood all over him. Will it change him? Of course, it will; we just don't know how. I won't live long enough to find out. He and his mom lived with me for part of his life, and I should know all about them, but I don't. They up and moved out, moved in with my son who won't so much as cross the street to say hi to me. Does that make me an example for all of America?

"When I rebuilt my cabin, I made sure it was a family place. Me and Danver took the kids out there all the time. Picnics, sleep-outs, hunting. That's where I taught my son how to shoot, and where Fulton learned to shoot. Go out there now and you'll see some of my rifles. The really good ones I store here at home, but I keep a few out there still. It's where they learned to be men, just like I did. Fulton still likes to spend time out at the cabin. When he goes on a drinking binge, he stays there until it passes. He and his buddies liked to have parties out there back when they were in high school. Good for them; it kept them out of real trouble in town. I'm pretty sure that's where he and Burelle made the baby. I wish Fulton would've married her, but he just didn't want to. She's a pretty good girl and a good mom to Random. But Fulton just didn't see it like that when he came back from Vietnam. He misses his son though, now that they're over at Hogan's. I don't know how that's going to work out, but things always do.

"Anyway, I hope I've given you what you needed for school, young fella. Even though I came from Poland, I want you to write that it was Germany. It sounds better today."

CHAPTER 21

Photos from the church shooting cover the surfaces of the police work room. Most were taken in the minutes and hours after the murders by a local photographer who doubles as the police and sheriff photographer. A dozen came from the Denver newspapers, shots that did not make it into the paper because of their graphic nature. The local crime scene photos are color pictures that show the bloody scene in its most vivid horror; they are obscene. Chief Russo studies each one at length before moving on to the next. Esch trails him recording the chief's comments and rearranging the photos as per his instructions. "Take that one and tack it to the wall with the other ones with the rifle. Put all the ones with the deceased boys on the small table but keep them separate from Mrs. Tuttle's." Russo walks and pauses, walks and studies. He's been doing this since the photos came in from Denver's crime lab where they were developed. "Why do you suppose he let the little boys live when he so eagerly shot the teenagers? It can't be just their ages. Was he planning on shooting the little boys too? Was there even a plan in that crazy head of his? God! I wish I could get into his mind."

Esch doesn't answer because she understands Russo isn't actually talking to her. He's working through the shooting out loud, trying to understand Robbie Hollins' motive, if he had one, or whether he was just crazy. Esch has theories, but she holds them close; Russo hasn't asked yet. She knew Robbie a little, as much as anyone on the force really had. He was reserved, a quiet kid who moved through the school system mostly unnoticed, ghostlike. He lived just down the street from Esch, and she babysat him years earlier. It was easy money. They watched television or played cards, and he didn't mind if her boyfriend came over for a while. Robbie seemed to like Fulton, even being a bit in awe of the high school football star. Esch studies one of the four photos of Robbie as he was being processed into the jail, and she wonders how things changed so drastically. Eight years and life flipped upon itself. Eagle Canyon, Colorado, will be forever changed; it will be linked to this terrible shooting.

Robbie Hollins' name will be remembered long after the victims' names are forgotten. TV and newspapers will avoid using Bradley's and Billy's names, ostensibly to protect their memory and preserve the privacy of the families, but it will only lead to their being consigned to oblivion, buried like their bodies. Mrs. Tuttle may have a local park named in her memory. When people speak of the tragedy, Robbie Hollins' name will come up. He was eighteen, died at age eighteen, the summer of his graduation, and he never seemed to be angry, so this is all unexplainable. Russo refuses the general consensus that the murders just happened or that Robbie had simply snapped. "Someone had to have known, or at least have had an indication." Since the murders the chief has interviewed the school counselor, Pastor Chamberlain, Robbie's boss at Safeway where he worked as a stock boy, his mother, and dozens of others who crossed Robbie's path. Russo hasn't been able to find Robbie's father, nor has he called from a faraway place to offer up information about his boy. A ghost, just like his son. Everyone called Robbie a shy boy, a good worker, a Christian, often disconnected. No one could have predicted this. "It was 'God's will.'" But it did happen.

Russo's mind races. Where did he get the rifle? Robbie's mother swears it isn't hers. They keep guns in the house. "Who doesn't?" she challenged. And the pistol Robbie carried in his belt that wasn't fired did belong to his mother, but not the rifle. An AK-47 military weapon. A thirty-clip, automatic rifle, built in a foreign country. Chief Russo walks over to the side table and picks it up. The M-16's counterpart in Vietnam. It has a good feel; Russo has fired one on the range and likes it. Not for hunting, but just to shoot. Russo does like the feel of a well-made rifle. Robbie fired six times, and two dozen cartridges remained to be used. "Used," Russo says softly, but loud enough for Esch to hear. Russo believes that if Robbie hadn't used the AK-47, he would have obtained another weapon for his carnage.

"Esch, I'm at the range a lot, and I never saw Robbie there. Did you ever hear of Robbie using a gun?"

"No, never." Esch holds a photo of Reverend Chamberlain praying over one of the slain teenagers. She finds herself still angry about the pastor's actions on Sunday morning. She returns the photo to its place among the pictures taken of the people who tried to help and comfort the victims, and then walks over to where the chief holds the AK-47. "I was in his house occasionally, mostly to babysit when he was about nine or ten. Mrs. Hollins kept their guns in the closet. I only know that because I would hang my coat up when I came. I've tried to remember how many guns and what kind, but it was just too long ago. There were several though. It was before I thought about being a police officer, before I had an interest in guns."

"It seems like so many of these families have no common sense about their guns. They don't lock them up; they keep them loaded. They're paranoid about break-ins. We have so little of that in Eagle Canyon, but if I ask them, they always tell me they've got to protect their home. They read about Chicago's and New York's violence or a gang killing in Los Angeles and think it's going to happen here. I tell people we have almost no violence here in our little town, and you know what their response is? They say, 'Well, it could happen. You never can be too careful.' I understand home protection. I do it too, but I don't keep the gun loaded." Russo shakes his head and sets the AK-47 back down on the table. "I'll take you to the range someday and let you shoot one of these, deputy. They're fun, but it's the only place they belong."

"Do you keep your service revolver loaded around the house, Chief?" asks Esch.

"Not loaded. The first thing I do when I get home is unload my weapon. I store it in the drawer next to the bed. My rifles are locked up in the gun cabinet, and the ammunition is in the closet." He pauses to consider his words. Then, he asks his deputy, "I suspect you do too?"

"Yes, this one," she replies as she touches her service revolver. "I don't fear a stranger though." Russo looks at her silently asking the follow-up question. "It's Fulton Tree," says Esch.

The chief nods. "Burelle mentioned that too." He pauses, looks at the photos, rearranges three of them, and then turns back to Esch. "Aren't you worried about your girls finding your gun? If they do, and it's loaded, I'll be investigating another tragedy." Russo is softly admonishing his young officer. "Your revolver is much more likely to be discharged accidently in the home than used to fend off an intruder. Or Fulton." Russo lets that sink in while he stares at Esch. "Has Fulton pulled a gun on you?"

Esch lies. "No, he's just . . . Fulton." She's surprised that Burelle told Russo about Fulton, since she keeps that chapter of her life bottled up. Esch rubs her forehead. "It's not guns per se. Fulton's just an angry guy. He always has been, but maybe more so since coming home from Vietnam. He acts like he's entitled to be angry, that the war or something gives him an extra right. It seems like we all excuse him for his fights, you know, the crazy veteran. He gets in trouble, gets in another fight at The Jungle, and Morvid comes and gets him. We never press charges. Does he even have a criminal record?"

Russo allows Esch's frustrations to sit with her for a moment while he considers her words. He walks deliberately to another table of photos before speaking. "He is entitled to a degree. No excuses, but a steady job would do wonders for him, I think."

"Isn't using Vietnam an excuse? It's been three years now."

"No, I don't see it that way. He's still young with a life ahead of him. There's still time."

"You keep trying to set him up with a job. He can't keep one. What he needs is a permanent cell in a prison far from here. It's not about Fulton anymore. It's about the safety of Burelle or some loser at the bar."

Russo shakes his head. He's not really interested in discussing Fulton Tree just now. His senses are focused on Robbie Hollins. "If it would have been an angry veteran or drunk who shot Bradley and Billy and Mrs. Tuttle, we might have understood. But it was

Robbie. How do we prevent that? How could we have predicted that?" He goes silent again and studies the photos. "Robbie worked at Safeway during high school; a steady job."

She turns back to a photo of Mrs. Tuttle lying on the floor covered with blood. Someone must have removed the blanket that protected her too late, hid the savagery of an hour earlier, so that photos could record the event in greater detail. This is a photo, like so many others, that never made the papers because it is too graphic. Protect the readers. Protect the victims. Tell everyone about what happened, but God forbid they actually see the gore.

"What do you see?" asks Russo.

"Robes. All of Robbie's victims were wearing robes. The three little boys weren't. I don't know if it means anything, but it just hit me. Robbie has his acolyte robe on, but he wasn't helping for that service, was he?" Esch hands the photo to Russo. "Reverend Chamberlain was wearing a robe."

"Hmm. He was screaming about wanting to find Reverend Chamberlain. Wouldn't he have known where to find him?" Russo hands the picture back to Esch. "Crazy. That's all I come up with. A crazy boy whose actions make no sense."

On the wall just over the chief's shoulder hangs an eight-by-eleven photo of Robbie Hollins, his graduation picture, the focal point of the exhibit. Robbie doesn't see Esch staring at him. His eyes didn't look directly at the camera. She wonders what he was seeing at the moment the photographer snapped the picture. She wonders if God will allow Robbie into Heaven since he killed people in His house. Russo stands at the point in the room where he can turn his eyes and see each display of evidence. The light entering the upper window above the table shines just to his right. A photographer might ask the police chief to move slightly to get into clearer focus.

"You can go on your patrol now, Esch. Leave the notes on the table and close the door behind you. You were a big help. Thanks."

For several minutes the big man is motionless, his eyes fixed on the photos of Billy and Bradley. The light from the window moves closer to where he stands. He takes a toothpick from his breast pocket. By habit, he cleans two or three gaps, slides it into his mouth to chew, and rests his hands on his hips. His eyes catch a random shot of Billy, partially hidden behind the closet door, lying on his side. Russo takes the toothpick from his mouth and mumbles questions to the two boys. "What did you do to make him do this to you? Weren't you all friends here in church? You served together. You must have. Why would he turn on you?" The boys don't answer his questions. Russo works his back teeth with the pick, which distorts his face. He moves to the photos of Robbie and picks one up. Damn, thinks the chief, he is wearing part of a robe.

# CHAPTER 22

Burelle now cooks for three even though Hogan doesn't usually arrive home from work until after seven: simple meals, hamburger-based, or pasta. Hogan likes steaks and lamb on special occasions, but his refrigerator is stocked with TV dinners, so Burelle's fresh meals replace some of those. His hours are longer than theirs by choice, but shorter than when he lived alone, and he seems not to need much sleep. Burelle watches television, where Random and Hogan read books. Random never minded the sound of the television at Morvid's house; he grew up with that sound. In the evening they would sit together, she is watching a drama and Random next to her with his book. At Hogan's house, as summer draws to a close and the aspen along the streets of Eagle Canyon are turning gold, orange, and red, Burelle's and Random's routine stays the same. Only their level of anxiety has changed.

In the second week of October, after Burelle tucks Random into bed, she and Hogan sit together. They were not always close for reasons Burelle never quite understood. Hogan's estrangement from Morvid and Fulton somehow transferred to Burelle and Random, but Random got into Hogan's heart over time, and Burelle came along. Hogan somehow understood that she needed at least one Tree to care, to look over her and the baby, and to possibly understand her precarious life, not as a Tree, but as the mother of the next generation Tree. Hogan discovered that he liked Burelle as a person, apart from just being his grandson's mother. She sacrificed a life of her own for her son, and Hogan understands that. She spoke little, but took a lot in. She lacked confidence, but Hogan thought he saw a method to her, a plan for living. But the lack of confidence and her fear of Fulton kept her locked up. Over time, he found Burelle to be imaginative and curious, even though they shared a common trait of quiet contemplation.

"I saw Chief Russo today, and he said you're doing good. He likes that you show up promptly after you've dropped Randy off at school." Hogan laughs. "He knows that he carried old man Carter about two decades too long as the janitor, but he couldn't just fire him. Russo's a pretty good guy with a good heart. He really does care for the people of this town." Hogan pauses. "His town." Again, he pauses. "I think more than anyone, except the four families who lost someone, he suffers more than anyone about the killings. I see it in his face; he's tired in a way, but he won't leave it alone. On one level he wants to understand Robbie. He refuses to accept that Robbie was simply crazy and move on. But more importantly, I think, Russo is trying to learn lessons about the shooting, so it won't happen again somewhere else. He wants to pass something on about this whole tragedy."

"It's natural to want to put it behind us, to not have to remember it each day. That can be so draining," says Burelle.

"I see that in you, you know. I understand it and wish I could do more." Hogan raises his head a little and looks over to Burelle. She smiles but says nothing. "Are you enjoying your work?" he asks.

"It's a good job. People are friendly and professional. I've never really been in that environment before. They have a purpose beyond a paycheck. I've been busy cleaning up places in the office that haven't seen a broom or a dust rag in years." Burelle smiles and laughs quietly. "I won't be there as long as Carter though." She stands up to turn off the TV and refill her coffee. "Want a cup?"

"No, I'll get one when I go out for my smoke."

When she returns, they sit in silence for a time, Burelle holding her coffee with both hands in front of her mouth. Finally, she asks, "How's your wife?"

"She's good. Her home is New Zealand, not here. We write."

"Do you miss her?"

"Every day, but she couldn't live here, not around Morvid and Fulton."

"I couldn't leave Random. He's my life."

Hogan leans forward towards Burelle. "Randy is not Fulton. How two people from the same roots can be so different is beyond me, but they are. Gertie tried to raise Fulton when I was in the nut house down the road, but he was a crazy boy. Gertie's a physical woman; she needs to be held and to hold. Fulton rejected all that. He yelled and screamed and hit. Fulton rejected any of the gentleness that Gertie offered, like he wasn't wired right at birth. I finally checked myself out, came back here, and sent her away. A person's got her own soul, and Fulton was ruining Gertie's. I couldn't allow that."

"You still love her, don't you?"

"Yes, very much."

"I hope I find someone who loves me like that in my life. So far, I never have." Burelle's dark eyes pierce the night, as if she can see better then. So much of her adult life has been spent in darkness.

"Why haven't you taken Random and left?" asks Hogan.

Burelle makes a high-pitched sound like a sarcastic laugh. "I left once. To Denver. Morvid came and got me, told me it was better that he showed up rather than Fulton. He told me Fulton would kill me if I ever left again. He even implied that he might do the same, because I couldn't take Random away from them. When I got back to his house, I paid the price with Fulton. He made Random sleep in the big house in the room next to him. I promised him I'd never leave again if he would only let Random come back to my part of the house." She doesn't divulge that Morvid betrayed her location and slapped her when he arrived to get her. "I'm twenty-three and I still don't know how to defend myself."

Hogan's jaw twitches. He wants to promise Burelle that he won't allow Fulton to hurt her again, but he isn't sure he can keep such a promise. "Burelle, there's meaning in suffering. Sometimes you have to forego happiness for meaning. It's not about the present, but about the future. You're a wise girl to understand that."

"Thank you for saying that. I accept it, but I don't understand it. I don't understand violence." She pauses. "Maybe that's not quite right. What I mean is that I kind of understand it, I just don't know how to respond to it." She pauses again. "Other than to cower. It's just how my families have always been."

They sit with their own thoughts for a time before Hogan speaks again. "Why don't you go check on Randy. I'll have my smoke and get that coffee, and then I want to tell you something." He stands and steps to Burelle, kisses her on the top of her head, and heads out the kitchen door to the back porch. Burelle watches him and wonders how a man can live apart from a woman whom he obviously loves dearly. She rises and climbs the stairs to Random's room. He sleeps soundly on his tummy with his head turned to the wall. Burelle sits gently next to her son, leans over and kisses his cheek, and then lays her hand on his head. "Thank you, Hogan, for this," she whispers.

Ten or so minutes later, Burelle hears the kitchen door close and Hogan pouring himself a coffee. She kisses Random once more and descends the stairs to join Hogan in the living room. He has warmed her coffee.

"The evenings are getting colder fast. Maybe I'll have to give up smoking for the winter." He smiles. "How's Randy?"

"He's good. He sure likes his room."

Hogan sips his coffee and leans forward toward Burelle. "Having you and Randy here has been nice. Different, but very nice. I've always talked to myself, sometimes out loud. Tinker has listened to all my thoughts, haven't you, girl." Hogan reaches down and scratches the old dog's neck. "Gertie used to laugh when she'd catch me talking out loud. We were opposites in so many ways, but good for each other. In New Zealand she would drag me to parties and gatherings. She was the center of any get-together, and I was like the wallflower. Here in Eagle Canyon, when we came back here to live before Fulton was born, it was different. She wasn't herself, and we kind of just stayed by ourselves here in this house." Hogan looks at Burelle, but his vision focuses on images of long ago. He catches himself and comes back to Burelle. "There are parts of my life that nobody here in Colorado knows about. Not my son, not my dad, nobody. Tonight, I'm going to tell you a few of those things. I trust you never to tell anyone until I'm long gone, and then you can tell

Randy about Grampa." Hogan breathes out heavily, lifts his coffee cup in a toast, nods, and takes a drink. Burelle reciprocates and smiles, indicating she's eager to hear.

Hogan opens his wallet and takes out a wrinkled photograph. He studies it for a moment and then hands it to Burelle. "That's my first family, my New Zealand family. After the war. You know a little about this, but not the important parts. After the war I had to return to the United States to muster out of the Navy, but Gertie and I had already married. As soon as I could, I went back to New Zealand. We lived with her family on the North Island. There's a great lake in the center of the country called Lake Taupo. It's an old volcano lake. Her family owns a farm a little northeast of that lake. They had fifty or sixty cows and operated a dairy mostly. They weren't rich, but they were comfortable. Gertie being Gertie, she got her family to take me in wholeheartedly, and I loved the farm lifestyle. I had a little problem adjusting to the earthquake tremors, but they taught me to be prepared for the worst. The biggest ones didn't happen around us; they were on the southern island, but we were aware. Once, when a tremor was happening and I was scared, Gertie laughed and told me to just spread my feet and keep balanced. She knew I was worried." Hogan sips his coffee and points to the photo.

"All those people in the back are Gertie's family. Farmers to the core, people of the soil. Me and Gertie are sitting down, and those two kids are our little boy and girl. Richie and Rebekkah. Reba for short." Hogan pauses to allow Burelle to catch up. "My New Zealand family."

Burelle runs her index finger over the photo softly. She knows the next part of his story is not going to be happy; she feels it in her chest. She finds the courage to look at her father-in-law and let him continue.

"Twins. We had celebrated their third birthday just a few days before that picture was taken. We were up at the region's fair in Rotorua. It was a great time. About a week after that, they were killed in a tractor accident. Grampa Taylor was giving them a ride on the old Fergie when it rolled over and crushed my kids. Mowing hay on a slope, not doing anything he hadn't done his whole lifetime, but this time it rolled. I shouldn't have allowed them to be riding, but it's what farm kids do." Hogan sniffles and rolls his lips inward. He exhales and slides his tongue between his teeth hoping not to cry. Still, tears form in the corners of his eyes. "Sorry. Even though it's been nearly thirty years ago, it's still pretty raw."

Burelle reaches over and takes Hogan's hand. "Oh, Dad, I'm so sorry." It's the first time Burelle has ever called Hogan dad.

"Gertie and I both sort of went into a depressed state after that. We promised each other we'd have more kids, just not for a while. We didn't blame Grampa Taylor, but he had broken his hip in the accident and just slipped away from guilt. He died within the year. We thought maybe some time away would be good for us, so we moved back here. A couple of years later, we had Fulton. She threw herself into being a mother; she loved him so much. The problem was that Fulton didn't seem to respond to her touch. He wasn't like Richie or Reba at all. I wasn't much help to her. I couldn't get past the accident. That's when I went to the Institute in Denver. I left Gertie alone to raise Fulton. I should say, alone to deal with Fulton. Whenever she'd come to visit me, I could see she was drowning, so I checked myself out and came back here. I wasn't any help to her, so that's when I decided to send her back to New Zealand. The promise was that I would join her, but I couldn't ever figure out what to do with Fulton. He's my responsibility. I couldn't just leave him here, and I wasn't going to take him to Gertie, so the years mounted, and we've been apart all these years."

When Hogan looks up again, Burelle sees that he has retreated into his eye sockets as if he's aged a decade in an evening. With her other hand she covers his and speaks. "I have a million questions, but I'll save most of them for later." She waits, but then asks, "How is Gertie? Does she still live with her family?"

Hogan smiles slightly while nodding. "She's good, and yes, she does. I guess she mostly runs the farm these days. It's grown. Everything she touches turns to gold. Well, except Fulton, but yeah, she's good. She tells me her life would be complete if only I was there, but I've still got this responsibility for my son. I can't just dump him on Morvid and this town. I'm the only one that has a semblance of control over him." Hogan pauses, begins to speak, and then pauses again. "Let me get it all out. When I sent Gertie away, she got angry. Even though Fulton had hurt her, she demanded to stay, begged to stay, but I wouldn't allow it. For several years we didn't write much, but neither of us took up with anyone else. I did write her when Fulton was about to graduate and go into the Army, and we started writing pretty regularly and making plans. I thought I'd join her while he was away, but for some strange reason, I fell into depression again. The Institute allowed me to stay weekends and most nights while I kept working at the school. Jesus! Working was all that kept me sane. And you and Randy seemed to be doing good. Then, Fulton came home, madder and wilder than before, and I convinced myself I had to stay and protect . . . you."

"I know. I wish there was another solution."

"I've tried, Burelle, and I keep running into obstacles. Anyway, there's something I want you to think about. I write Gertie about you. She knows you and especially Randy. There's a link between you and Gertie. She wants you and Randy to come to New Zealand, to live with her on the farm. It would be a place where Fulton couldn't get to you."

Burelle watches as Hogan begins to emerge from the caverns of his eyes, as his expression becomes more optimistic. Forward looking. The thought of leaving Eagle Canyon for somewhere, to something, rather than fleeing to escape intrigues her. She knows she would be fleeing, but this seems different than running to Denver. "Would you go too?"

"Yes. Not on the same day, but soon after." Hogan has thought this out. "I tell myself that it's not fair to Morvid to be left in charge of Fulton, but sometimes life is fair. It just takes time for fair to work itself out. When I was growing up, Morvid drank heavily. He beat me every weekend. He'd take me out to that goddam cabin and let me have it. Then, when we'd return, he'd tell my mom how much fun we had. That's when I stopped calling him Pop and began using Morvid. It was my subtle way of showing disrespect. I think that's why he excuses Fulton for his drinking and fighting; he did it and outgrew it, and now he thinks Fulton will do the same." Hogan shakes his head. "But he won't. Fulton's sick. He needs to be institutionalized. I'm working on that."

Both Burelle and Hogan go quiet for a moment. Burelle stands, as if she forgot something, then sits down again. "How soon?"

"Not long. We'd need to get you and Randy passports, but beyond that, I'd just drive you to the airport one anonymous day and put you on a plane. Don't tell anyone, not even Randy. Keep everything a secret, and then one day you're no longer here. That's why you and I can't leave together, because someone might put us together in New Zealand. But if I wait a month or two after that and get Fulton taken care of, I can tell Morvid that I'm going back to Gertie, and he'd believe it. He's a rich man with lots of resources, and if he thought you were in New Zealand, he might come after you. For Randy."

"Is it too early for me to have a dream, a hopeful dream?"

"No, Burelle, it's not too early. In fact, it's way past time."

§

Two nights later, while Random sleeps and Hogan works late, Burelle enters Hogan's bedroom, unlocks the drawer, and removes the revolver. She sits on Hogan's bed with only the light from the hallway on, cautiously holding the gun like it is a small bird with a broken wing. She rolls it into her right hand, trying to fit it comfortably into her palm. She stands, eyes herself in the dresser mirror, raises the pistol, and points it at those eyes.

CHAPTER 23

Chief Russo understands Burelle's fear of Fulton, although he hadn't considered it before. He's disappointed in himself for accepting the Trees' story that Burelle drinks heavily. She's been a conscientious worker with no signs of a drinking problem. Burelle's residence at Morvid Tree's house for so long was a topic of Eagle Canyon gossip, but only because Random Tree is Fulton's son and Fulton never married Burelle. Morvid's big house sits semi-secluded with a large yard, big trees, and a stately fence. What occurs inside that fence stays private. Fulton's behavior outside those walls provides enough fodder anyway. Despite Burelle's native status in Eagle Canyon, the town folk don't know much about her. Before Russo hired her as the department custodian, she kept to herself, worked odd jobs to earn a few dollars, mostly as a waitress or house cleaner, and raised her son. Russo hadn't considered Fulton's teenage years. He chews on it for a few days and then decides to talk with Morvid. The chief knows Morvid will deny any allegation and will relay the information to Fulton if it is spoken as a charge, so Russo knows to tread lightly. Fulton is a hothead, but outside of bar fights, he's never done anything else to anyone, at least to the chief's knowledge or the records indicate. Fulton has been the pampered grandson of a rich, retired banker. Russo always assumed that Fulton would grow out of his adult adolescence in time, like so many other men who serve in the military right out of high school, but it's taking longer than it should.

§

Chief Russo parks in front of the large red brick house, radios the dispatcher to tell her where he will be for the next hour or so, and walks the long stone path up to the oversized, wooden door. He notes that the Tree mansion has been allowed to deteriorate some, and Russo wonders why. Morvid can no longer do the work, but he certainly has the money to pay to get it done. And there's Fulton. The police chief rings the bell.

"Chief, you've had a busy couple of weeks. Come in and sit awhile. Can I get you a coffee?" Morvid pours two cups, and the two men sit at Morvid's kitchen table. "What brings you over?"

Russo lays his cap on the table, which has numerous cigarette burns on its surface, and rubs his thinning hair. "It has been something, that's for sure. Morvid, I'm worried about Fulton. His son gets shot at, he gets clubbed over the head on that same day over at The Jungle, and now I hear he's lost another job. I'm concerned he might not be coping well, and I wondered if I could help." Russo runs his forefinger along the edge of the table and follows his finger with his eyes before looking up to the older man.

"Well, that's mighty nice of you. He does need a job, otherwise he gets antsy. Most people do, and Fulton's no different. I wish he would've hung onto that one in Denver that you got for him. You don't happen to have an opening in your department, do you? Maybe one with a car?"

Chief Russo laughs, knowing Morvid is mostly kidding, but the chief also assumes Morvid believes his grandson is normal. Maybe he is. Morvid didn't get to be one of the richest men in the county by being a fool. "Fulton can be a bit ornery, that's for sure. I appreciate that you took over when he and Hogan broke apart. You've been good for him." Russo sips his coffee and looks over the kitchen. "I understand Burelle moved out and took Random. How's Fulton handling that?"

"Oh, it's mostly okay. Fulton seems to have a new girl down in Denver. He never had a problem getting a girl. That Burelle's gone doesn't bother him, he's glad for that, but he does miss his boy some. So do I. At first, I thought he might go get Random, but we talked and it's okay." Morvid puts his finger in his coffee and swirls it around, not flinching even though the coffee is hot. "Did you happen to catch the man who blindsided Fulton at the bar?" asks Morvid.

"Nobody seems to want to rat anyone else out. You know the code of the bar. Everyone who even admits that he was there says he was in the head taking a piss and didn't see anything. Fulton told me after it happened that it was just one of those things, and I wasn't to worry about it." Chief Russo shifts in his chair to stretch his shoulders. "Do you think it might do Fulton some good if he talked to one of the counselors connected with the police department? Several of the families have utilized their services to talk out some of their concerns about the shooting." Russo fidgets with a placemat as he speaks. He isn't comfortable suggesting this, knowing how Fulton would respond, but the chief hopes Morvid can get Fulton to go.

"He doesn't need a shrink. He's fine. Once he found out that his boy wasn't hurt, he was all right. The only thing that got him riled up was when Robbie killed himself and won't have to pay any consequence for his actions. That didn't sit well with Fulton. Robbie gets to decide his own fate, but those boys and that lady sure don't get to."

"Yeah, that bothers a lot of us. I sure would have liked to talk with Robbie more and find out why he did it. He was a quiet boy, but nobody ever saw this coming. I can understand your frustration of not knowing. We all are."

Morvid straightens in his chair, leans forward toward the police chief, and gets his eye. "Robbie's parents ought to be ashamed. It's a dad's responsibility to raise his son the right way, and it's obvious he didn't. I remember back during The Great War when my cabin was shot up so bad that my Pap had to burn it down. Those boys that did it died in the war, but I still held their pop responsible. I shoved a gun in his face when I returned from France. Maybe Mr. Hollins should have shoved a gun in his son's face and told him to behave."

Morvid's comment raises the hair on Russo's neck. Russo reaches across the table and lays his big hand on the old man's arm. "Settle down. Robbie's dad hasn't been around in years, and I haven't been able to locate him. The boy was raised by his mother, and she's devastated. More than anyone, she wants to know why. I think you can appreciate the difficulty a single parent has." Russo's eyes help transmit his message.

"She should have known, should have checked his room for guns or something. She should have done more." Morvid's words are not as forceful as his early comment, and he seems, to the police chief, to be retreating some while saving face.

Russo moves carefully. "Maybe, but I know when my boys got to a certain age, I didn't search their rooms. We grew up with guns. I taught them how to use them early, and then I trusted them to use them only like I taught them. I imagine you did the same with Fulton."

Morvid goes to another place for a moment. At eighty years old, the chief imagines that the old man has several caves to crawl in and out of. Russo waits. Finally, Morvid returns. "I taught Fulton how to shoot some, but not much else about guns. That was Hogan's job, but he went down the mountain to the funny farm for a few years. Gertrude could have done it, I suppose, but I never did. When Hogan came home, she left, and I think he didn't trust himself with guns, so Fulton pretty much learned with his friends."

"Does he have many guns now?" asks Russo.

"I think so, but I don't know how many. I don't go into his room. He's a grown man; he's earned his privacy. He fought for the country in Vietnam. He deserves a gun. He loves to hunt, especially them birds in eastern Colorado. Every time he goes, he comes back with a hundred or more."

The chief pushes his chair back in preparation to leave. "I've drunk enough of your bad coffee, and I need to get back to work before they think I'm off sleeping in my car somewhere. I thank you for your hospitality, Morvid. I want you to let me know if I can do anything for you or Fulton. I know this has been tough, and you've both held a lot in. You Trees are tough, tougher than me, that's for sure."

The two men stand and walk out to the patrol car. "I appreciate you coming by, Chief, but Fulton's doing okay. I'll tell him you stopped by. If you hear of a job he could fill, let me know." The men shake hands, and Russo drives off. Morvid watches the car until it turns south toward Main Street. Then, he opens the gate and starts walking in the direction of his son's house, hoping to get a glimpse of his great-grandson.

§

In the two months that have passed since the murders, Police Chief Russo has not lived an hour without thinking about why it happened. Today, he drives to the Lutheran church where the shooting occurred. He parks on the street, turns off the engine, and scans the church setting like he's done every day since the tragedy. Of all people, he thinks, why Robbie? Russo gets out and walks to the church parking lot, to the spot where Robbie's car was parked on that Sunday. He's always had a feel for his work, what his wife calls his "sick sense," but he hasn't channeled anything on this case. Everything he knows has come from the investigation, not intuition, but none of that has answered why.

He slides his boot across the asphalt as if scratching an itch on the lot. His head is down in thought. It was something about the church—maybe. He looks to the steeple and walks toward the church wing where the Sunday school classes are held, a walk he's taken before as he traces Robbie's most likely path. Church had ended, and the congregants must have been milling around, but nobody recalls seeing Robbie take this walk with the weapon. Wouldn't it have been obvious? Was Robbie a ghost on this walk like he was throughout most of his short life?

The chief unlocks the door, a door that was unlocked that Sunday, but now is kept secure. The proverbial barn door. Russo examines the key he obtained in order to gain entrance for the ongoing investigation. The key. Again, he berates himself for not seeing this coming, but he shakes his head to reprimand himself. "You couldn't have known, Roos," he mutters aloud. The hallway is wide and bright. If Robbie had passed anyone, they would have recognized him and said something. Russo trails his hand along the wall as he walks to Mrs. Tuttle's room. It remains sealed, by his orders, but again, he has a key.

Inside, the grizzly details have been left untouched. Crime scene evidence. Russo's been criticized for this, but he won't order the room scrubbed until it tells him more, until it reveals its secrets. He and the room are competitors, and patience is required in this contest. He moves to the corner where Mrs. Tuttle shielded the younger boys, and he crouches like she might have. His weight makes this move difficult; it would have for the overweight Sunday school teacher too. Robbie must have stared into her eyes before he fired. Did he see her eyes or just a figure? Did he fire at real people or had he checked out by then? What did Mrs. Tuttle think when Robbie shot the altar boys? Russo can imagine what she felt, protecting her own. Russo understands; he was Bradley Arnold's godfather.

The chief stands and moves to where he thinks Robbie stood. "Where's Pastor Chamberlain?" Russo asked the reverend why Robbie might have been so adamant about seeing him, but the minister didn't know. If it was the reverend that Robbie so wanted to see, why then did he go into Mrs. Tuttle's room where the pastor wouldn't be? Robbie should have been able to see the reverend at the front door of the church greeting the parishioners. Chief Russo has an answer, the answer that the experts in Denver gave him, but he doesn't want to believe it. "Face it, Chief. The boy acted irrationally; he was seeing a psychiatrist for a reason. It was simply a crazy action."

Russo faces toward the corner where Mrs. Tuttle and the young boys crouched. He pretends to be startled by the voice of one of the altar boys. Did he simply kill them because he was surprised? Did he turn and fire without thinking? Did that set in motion a chain of events leading to this massacre? Why then shoot the older boys twice? Why didn't he stop when Mrs. Tuttle tried to help him? Why didn't he shoot Random? He talked to Random first in a calm voice before demanding to see Pastor Chamberlain. Then, he lowered his rifle and walked out.

What if Robbie never meant to shoot anyone, but just wanted to be helped? Robbie can't tell him now, and the chief has combed every inch of the boy's room in search of a note that he might have left. Russo scans the room again, wanting one more view. He goes to the corner where the young boys hid behind Mrs. Tuttle and sits down. The chief, at over two hundred and fifty pounds, tries to see the shooter from the eyes of an eight-year-old boy who didn't act afraid, but must have been terrified. Russo squints to where Robbie stands. Why couldn't Robbie go home? What was Random thinking when he ordered Robbie to go home? Did the sound of a voice bring Robbie back to the present? Why hadn't Mrs. Tuttle's voice accomplished the same thing? Russo sits still; tries to channel Random at that moment. Random. Random. What did you do to keep Robbie from splattering your brains all over the room like he did Bradley and Billy?

Russo stands awkwardly and scans the room again. A closet, some cabinets, tables and chairs. He looks back to the closet. He's searched it before and found just a few vestments hanging; it was mostly empty when it should have been used for storage. In the corner are a broom and vacuum cleaner. It's not a large closet, but a man could stand in it. Maybe.

§

Back in the parking lot, Ollie Eastman leans against the chief's patrol car smoking a cigarette. Eastman retired from the military in '73 and took a job at Morvid's old bank. People around town call him 'Colonel,' his final rank, and he and Russo drink coffee on Friday mornings. With three other men, they discuss the Broncos, politics, and local events.

"Hey, Roos." Eastman straightens and steps to the chief to shake his hand. "Still pondering why, huh?" He drops his cigarette butt and steps on it.

"Yeah, Colonel. Not getting anywhere though." Russo pats Eastman on the shoulder and shakes his head. "I keep hoping for Robbie's secret to reveal itself suddenly, that if I put myself in his shoes, maybe I'll understand."

Eastman nods as a good friend does when listening to the concerns of his buddy, but it's more. "You just need to ask anyone in town; they'll tell you why Robbie did it." He's joking and Russo understands. "Roos, maybe I can help you a little. I heard through the grapevine that you're trying to find out where Robbie got the Kalashnikov." Eastman looks to the church steeple, and then returns to the chief. "I'm embarrassed about this, but you need to know." He pauses again. "I sold it to him this summer."

The two men stare at each other, searching for an opening. Finally, the chief asks, "How'd you know Robbie?"

Eastman steps back to the hood of the patrol car to lean against it for support. He lights another cigarette. "His mom and I were seeing each other for a while." He doesn't have to look up to know that Russo disapproves. Their wives spend time together and share a passion for canasta and shopping. Eastman continues. "Carol was worried about her son, you know, not having any friends, being a loner and all, so I volunteered to take him shooting. We didn't go to the range. We just went up to one of the old mines and shot up the place. He really liked the 47, and afterwards, he opened up just a little. I took him up there a second time, and he asked if he could take the weapon home and clean it. I let him, and a few days later, I sold it to him. Two hundred bucks. I have another one." The colonel goes silent, and Russo knows Eastman understands his error. Still, the chief wants to grab his friend by the lapels and shake the shit out of him. His jaw tightens.

"Fuck, Ollie," he mutters. The chief walks away from Eastman with his hand on the back of his neck. He turns back. "Are you still seeing Carol Hollins?"

"No. I broke that off a few weeks before the shooting. I haven't talked with her since." Eastman finally looks his friend in the eye. "I know I screwed up. I've been afraid to talk to you. I haven't told anyone about the weapon, and when I thought about it, I'm pretty sure Carol didn't know Robbie had it."

Russo swears again. "Of all people, Ollie, you should have known not to put a weapon in the hands of a kid who's not right. That's irresponsible, dammit. Didn't the Army teach you that?" It's a rhetorical question. "Shit! An AK-47 might be fun as hell to fire, but it's a military weapon; it's not for civilians, and it's certainly not for an unstable young man." Russo turns again and walks even farther off. He stares at the section of the church where the shootings occurred. Two little girls exit the door with Pastor Chamberlain. All three wave. Russo pivots back to the colonel. "You're going to need to stop by my office later and fill out a statement. I'll do what I can to keep this quiet. You'd have saved me a lot of valuable time if you'd have told me sooner." He starts to say something else, maybe dress down his friend again, but catches himself. "Get out of here, Ollie."

§

Russo sits at his desk holding a single photograph of the church room taken before any of the bodies were removed. It's the one photo he keeps coming back to because it shows the carnage in its starkest gore. He's interrupted by a soft rap at his open door. His dispatcher pokes her head in.

"Chief, you've got a phone call from a Chicago policeman. Captain Rowan. It's long distance."

Yes, it is, thinks Russo, a long, long distance. "Transfer it in here, please." Matt Rowan was Russo's partner when he worked on the Chicago police force, a man of intelligence and common sense. Also, he was about the funniest man Russo ever knew. No one on the force or in the streets escaped his subtle skewers. Russo stayed on the Chicago force an extra year out of respect for Rowan. The best cop. Russo picks up the phone, "Well, Matt, what have I done to get a call from you? It's been a few years."

"Hell, Roos, you went and got yourself famous with your town's church shooting. It's settled down some, but there for a while, you were the most quoted lawman in America. Never knew you were so erudite."

"I don't know what that word means."

"Wordy, but in a smooth sort of way." Rowan laughs. "Just called to see if you're doing okay, partner."

There's a pause. Then, Russo answers. "Yeah, I'm okay. The town's having a tough time, and I can't, for the life of me, figure out why the boy did it, but I'm okay."

"You're probably out of practice with big city crime. You

know, with the violent, crazy, fun stuff that we see every day here. Remember?"

"Yeah," answers Russo, "I remember."

"Three, huh?" It's a rhetorical question. Rowan knows how many were killed. "The young boys gotta be hard."

"They were. Still are. One of them was my godson. I see his dad most every week."

"The missis okay?"

"Yeah, she knew the people too. She worries about me. How about you, Matt?"

"Jaded. Hell, Roos, this happens every day in Chicago. One or two at a time. Fifteen to twenty each week. Nearly a thousand a year, and thousands more who are shot, but don't die. Twenty times more. All bloody."

"I remember," says Russo.

"I guess to become a celebrity like you, the killings have to take place in a church, a house of God, and come in multiples. If it's associated with drugs or poverty or gangs, nobody gives a shit. Shoot someone in the suburbs, and every TV station in the city wants the story."

Each man on his end shakes his head. They talk for another ten minutes, catching up on their own kids, Russo asking about some of the other officers that he once worked with, both avoiding anything more about the church murders.

"Well, Roos, I gotta hang up. I'm using the company dime here. Just wanted to let you know I was thinking about you."

"I appreciate that, Matt, I really do." Russo puts the phone in the cradle. He nods his head and smiles. There are those out there who understand. Not many, but a few.

§

Eastman enters the police station after dark, after regular work hours, at a time when few people will notice his movements. He wears a dark blue baseball hat with Vietnam emblazoned on the front. He makes small talk with the dispatcher before sitting down in Chief Russo's office for what he believes will be a lecture.

"Coffee?" asks Russo.

"Nah. Too late. It'd just keep me awake."

Russo pours himself a cup and then settles into his padded desk chair. It's official business, but it's between good friends, and Russo is good at congenial interviews and of getting information from his townspeople. He sips his coffee, sniffles, pulls out a legal pad, and asks again. "Are you sure you don't want a cup? Pretty good."

Ollie smiles and shakes his head. "You don't have any scotch in that lower drawer, do you?"

"No, but maybe we can go get a beer later." Russo reaches over and squeezes his friend's shoulder. "What did you make of Robbie when you spent time with him?"

"I gotta tell you, Roos, he was no monster like much of the town now believes. Far from it. If he became a beast, then it's because the devil entered into him. Robbie was painfully shy, maybe because he was funny looking. He sure didn't inherit any of his mom's good looks. Robbie had that angular face. It seems like every feature had its own agenda." Eastman pauses to reflect for a moment. Russo remembers his own description of Robbie. Unpleasant. Russo used the word to a Denver cop two days after the shooting. Eastman continues. "I felt sorry for him at first, but after I got him to talk to me a little, I realized what he looked like didn't really matter. You know how in the Army all those recruits look so homely and scared at first? That's what Robbie reminded me of, and in time you get past that and see the person, but I'm sure he saw it every morning in the mirror before school. He had a hard time making eye contact, but I think I earned his trust a little bit, and he got so he would look at me, especially when I reminded him of it. Not having a dad around hurt him. I had to teach him simple things, like how to shake hands. He would just put his out there for me to squeeze. I had to teach him a firm grip, to hold it for just a moment, to look a man in the face, to nod, to say 'Nice to meet you' or some such. Roos, he didn't really know how to talk to an adult. Imagine living in a town where no one acknowledges you. He was a part of Eagle Canyon, he was born here, one of our tree's branches, but he didn't fit in anywhere, it didn't seem." Eastman is leaning forward as he speaks.

"What did you talk to him about?"

"His demeanor would suggest that he felt sorry for himself, but I never got the feeling that he did when we talked. He knew baseball; he was a big Braves fan and knew all kinds of statistics about major leaguers. He asked about things around town, about school, about the military. He was a curious kid. His mom was floored that he talked to me so openly. He was a lot smarter than people gave him credit to be."

"Did he ever say anything that suggested he might be violent?"

"No, at least I didn't think so at the time. I even asked him about what he wanted to do with his life, and he said he had some things, but he also didn't want to leave his mom alone. He mentioned that he might want to be a policeman or a soldier or something like that, but I got the sense he hadn't thought much about his future." Eastman ponders his last words and then adds, "He was just a kid who was struggling to get by each day, and he couldn't focus on the future. Mostly, he just seemed sad. I've played those conversations over in my head, trying to remember something important. The closest I can come is something he said about other kids like him who struggle in school, about kids who needed to make a mark. It didn't come off as a threat at the time though."

Russo bites his lower lip and looks down at his notes. "There're so many kids like the one you described, Colonel. We need programs for kids like these. How can we tell?"

Ollie Eastman shakes his head. "I'm not sure we can, Roos. I'm not sure we can. Robbie couldn't even connect with his mom."

The two men sit in silence, their thoughts unknown to the other. When Russo is bothered by a particular police dilemma, he talks it over with his wife or the sheriff in Leadville, a man with similar historical and physical traits, in charge of a similar mountain, mining town. One of them always provides some insights, but on this neither his wife nor the Leadville sheriff have been able to assuage his concerns. The case is solved, but the why has not revealed itself, and there are no indications that it will.

The colonel scoots his chair back. "Roos, I think I've told you all I know. I should have come to you that first week, but I was ashamed. If you have any more questions, give me a call. You know I feel bad about this. I know I really screwed up selling Robbie that rifle, but he'd have found another. Anybody can get whatever he wants so easily, you know that." Eastman stands, nods at the seated police chief, turns, and walks toward the door. "I'll take a rain check on that beer. I need to go home and patch up my marriage, if I can. Thanks anyway."

Russo sits for another hour. Robbie got a gun, but the two boys he shot grew up with guns too. My boys had guns. I love to shoot. The chief keeps returning to the mental health of Robbie Hollins— and the absence of a father. Russo has talked with several experts in Denver, read articles on mental illness, and tried to learn all he could about the public attitudes toward those labeled as crazy. Eagle Canyon treated Robbie like a textbook case. We isolated him, rejected him, called him names, and generally forced him to think less of himself. It's so complicated. An unbalanced young man with access to automatic weapons. Russo doesn't have the answer. He slams his palm onto his desk. "You still had no reason to kill those people, Robbie, no fucking reason!" Simultaneously, Russo spins out of his chair and sweeps his notes off the desk and onto the floor.

CHAPTER 24

Strong winter winds race down the canyon in a seeming hurry to get to Denver, chasing the last golden aspen leaves from their ashen branches. Snow follows on the wind's tail, bringing the first measurable amount to Eagle Canyon. The snow is late this year. Burelle stands framed in the front window holding her coffee mug, watching the leaves swirl in the yard. She waits for Random and Hogan to return from trick-or-treating. She feels safer at Hogan's house, but not entirely safe when she is there alone. She knows Fulton's dark side; she remembers the pain of his blows, his hair-pulling, the ridicule, the forced sex at Morvid's after he returned from Vietnam. Before Vietnam, when they were in high school, Esch was Fulton's girlfriend, and she was Esch's best friend. Esch was petite and cute; she still is. Burelle was tall. Sophomores. It was after a football game from which Fulton had been suspended, and they had driven out to the cabin in late October to allow Fulton to let off some steam. He could drink a beer or two before the game and not let it affect his play. "I'm the best player on the team, goddammit." He was angry at the coach, at his teammates, at some unknown rat, at stupid people who didn't deserve to live, at his mom and dad who didn't love him; especially at his mom who had deserted him. "Fucking bitch!"

Esch tried to calm him down, but she made the mistake of defending Gertrude. "She must have just missed her family in New Zealand too much. I'm sure she loved you. Maybe it was Hogan's illness."

"How the fuck would you know? You never knew her." Fulton grabbed one of his rifles and went outside and began firing aimlessly into the forest. When he had emptied the clip, he came back inside for another magazine and repeated his actions. Esch told him she was going to leave him at the cabin and drive home and take Burelle with her. That's when Fulton pointed the rifle at her. He ordered her to leave, but Burelle had to stay. When Esch got back to Eagle Canyon, she realized she had made a mistake. It was out of fear, but a mistake nevertheless. She drove back to the cabin and found Fulton sitting on a wooden bench smoking dope, nearly passed out. Inside, Burelle sat on the floor, gently swaying back and forth. Esch knelt down and took Burelle's head into her arms. "I'm sorry. I'm sorry." That's all Esch could say. There was no consoling Burelle. Difficult as it was to get Burelle off the floor, Esch finally managed and then walked her to the car, leaving Fulton lying in the dirt next to the bench passed out. Esch never dated Fulton again.

This is what Burelle remembers when the darkness envelops her. She has Random, her boy born out of such evilness. Good from bad. Wonderful from awful. When her friends ask, when anyone asks for that matter, her stock answer is, "It was high school, and we do stupid things. I was young and things happened. It wasn't supposed to, but it did, and now I have Random."

Burelle sat near the top of her class, but she didn't graduate. Only her mother was around when Random was born. Her mother didn't stay long. Burelle remained in the trailer next to the interstate for over a year. Later, she moved in with Morvid when Fulton went to Vietnam. She prayed that he would be killed and never return. God didn't grant that wish. Like so many others.

§

Esch works the night shift for Halloween, and Burelle babysits Esch's twins, something she does occasionally when Esch's parents are out of town. Esch married while in college, the community college in west Denver where she earned her law enforcement diploma. Her husband, a highway patrolman who taught one of her classes, divorced her shortly after the twins were born, and Esch moved back to Eagle Canyon, back in with her parents. Lexi and Sarah are two and a few months, petite like their mother, and unaware of the summer's tragedy. Esch shelters them and they are too young to ask.

Hogan cut back working nights when Burelle and Random moved in with him. He informed the school he was getting too old for that nonsense and joked that his bed was more comfortable than the cot in the boiler room. Lexi and Sarah call him Uncle Hogan.

Chief Russo gives Esch time before her shift to take her girls trick-or-treating, and they finish just before the snow begins to fall. Their pumpkins aren't nearly as full as Random's will be three hours later. Still, they collect enough candy before dinner to last until Thanksgiving if it is rationed appropriately. Small towns go all out for Halloween. Esch drops them off with Burelle, since her parents are at a party in Denver, and begins her Halloween patrol. Random and Hogan are out for his trek, but the blowing snow forces him and his grandpa back early, before they are able to hit the expensive houses on the hill where the best candy is passed out. Hogan doesn't mind. Random charges in ahead of his grandpa just after darkness falls; both have snow on their coats. The boys giggle as they dump Random's candy on the table. Burelle hugs him before he sits down to sort his stash. She dishes up hotdogs with macaroni and cheese, and they settle in for the first night of winter. Random continues to wear his Chewbacca costume, minus the rubber mask, confusing the twins with his Star Wars jargon. Older trick-or-treaters brave the snow and continue to ring the doorbell until past nine. By then, over six inches of snow has piled up.

The extended family gathers in front of the TV, all five on Hogan's old, high-backed, colonial couch. The three children each clutch a blanket, Random sharing his with his mother as he sits on her lap, Lexi and Sarah entangled in pink and purple blankets and each other. The kids fall asleep quickly, as does old Tinker on Hogan's feet. Hogan rearranges himself because Tinker will now sleep through the night, an unusual dog that sleeps through thunder on the scariest night. Hogan pssts to Burelle to get her attention. He points to his dog, "It's Halloween and nothing's going to wake her now. I guess trick-or-treating did her in too." Later, Hogan dozes, but Burelle stays awake to the television, wanting to remember this night, this scene, the kids' excitement, Random in his costume.

While Burelle moves around straightening up, the phone rings. "Hello," answers Burelle just after ten.

"Hi, babe. It's me. I'm just checking on the girls. It looks like it could be a long night in the county. Lots of cars are pulling off the interstate and getting stuck in our little town. Are the girls doing good?" asks Esch.

"No problem. They're asleep on the couch. Hogan read them a few stories, but I think it was the anticipation and walking that did them in. I managed to have them eat a little dinner and not so much candy. I saved you the yellow jellybeans. Are you actually driving in this storm?"

"A little. Chief Russo has us riding in pairs, mostly behind the snowplow. We stop to dig out the stranded cars or give the people rides if we can't get their cars unstuck. We're more of a taxi service tonight. It's terrible out, but I think we'll be done after midnight; maybe one. There won't be school, so you and Hogan can sleep in."

"Hogan sleep in? That'll be the day." Burelle and Esch exchange small talk for a few minutes while Esch eats dinner at the station.

"I need to go, but I want to ask a favor. Could the girls spend the night? I'd hate to have to bundle them up in this weather and take the chance that I'd get stuck too."

"No problem. Nobody's going anywhere. You can come here when you get off and stay too. The girls would wonder where you are when they wake up." Hogan comes in just after Burelle hangs up. He's been shoveling snow off the porches and sidewalks, hoping to stay ahead of the mounting snow piles. Burelle tells him Esch's news and helps with his coat. "You've been smoking out there. You remember this is your house, don't you? You don't have to leave to have a cigarette."

"The kids don't need the smoke. Gertie didn't like it either. Besides, it makes me cut back when I don't smoke inside. That's a good thing. Let's watch the weather and see what they're predicting for tonight and tomorrow."

One more request for candy, from three teenage boys, comes

around eleven, and Burelle admonishes them for being out so late in such conditions. Hogan wonders out loud what the trick would be if they didn't receive their treat. Burelle carries Random from the couch into his bed, or to the hole in the wall that is Chewbacca's bed for tonight. She lays his lightsaber next to him. She kisses him goodnight, pulls a blanket up to his chin, and slides the curtain across the cubby hole. Hogan rearranges the twins, moving each to opposite ends of the couch, and pours himself a scotch from a plastic bottle.

"I'm glad this night is over," he says. "It's an overdone holiday."

"You're just getting to be an old fuddy-duddy." Burelle reaches for his glass and takes a sip of his scotch. She scrunches up her face in disgust. "I'm glad I don't drink. Esch will be coming in at some time tonight. I thought I'd put out an extra blanket, so she can nestle in between her girls. She's going to be one tired lady after tonight."

"You go to bed, Burelle. I'm going to stay up and read. If any more kids come around, I'll shoo them away." Burelle leans in and kisses her sort of father-in-law on the forehead. She turns off the porch light as a sign to trick-or-treaters that this house is closed and locks the front door on her way to her room.

§

Headlights flash through the front windows around one-fifteen, and Hogan gets up to turn on the porch light to make it easier for Esch. Four more inches of snow have fallen since he last shoveled. He walks back to the couch to re-cover Lexi who has thrown off her blanket. The knock at the door is excessive, but then he remembers he has forgotten to unlock it. "Just a minute." Simultaneously, he unlocks the door and turns the handle for Esch.

A large man in a black duster and Darth Vader mask bursts in. The door's side rail strikes Hogan at his temple, knocking him to the floor. "Where's Random? Where's my son?" the man demands.

Stunned, Hogan staggers to his feet only to be knocked to the floor again by the bigger man. Fulton Tree lifts the mask from his face and tosses it at Hogan's feet. "I'm not messing around tonight.

121

I'm taking Random back to the house." The two girls start crying and the upstairs hall light blinks on. "Shut the fuck up!" Fulton screams at the little girls. "Burelle, I want my son."

"He's not here, Fulton. He's spending the night with a friend. You can check his room." Burelle has not shown herself, but she can see Fulton. "His room is the first one at the top of the stairs."

Fulton grew up in this house and knows the layout. He mounts the stairs two steps at a time and pushes open Random's door. "Son, it's your dad. I've come to take you home." When he gets no answer, he turns on the bedroom light and looks at the empty bed. He steps back into the hall and demands to know where Random is.

Burelle continues to conceal herself, but the door to Hogan's room is ajar. "I told you he isn't here. I've got a gun, Fulton, and I'll use it, so help me God, so back down the stairs and get out of here."

Standing at the bottom of the stairs, Esch aims her service revolver at Fulton. When she arrived moments earlier and saw Fulton's truck and an open door, she knew. "If she doesn't shoot you, asshole, I will. Walk slowly and don't startle me." As Fulton descends the stairs, Esch steps back cautiously. Hogan lies unconscious on the floor near the door. "Don't touch him, Fulton. Just open the front door and get outside. Backup is on the way." Fulton does as ordered but his eyes leer at Esch. When he stumbles off the porch and onto the snow-covered sidewalk, he turns back.

"Pretty brave with that gun, bitch. You won't always have it, you know. Then, you'll get it." Fulton turns suddenly back to the street when he hears the siren. The red and blue flashing lights follow close behind. "I see your pimp has showed up."

From behind, Burelle places her hand on Esch's shoulder. "Move aside, Escher. I've got this." Burelle steps past the officer and raises Hogan's pistol, bringing her left hand onto the revolver for support. Her grip is firm and steady. She slides her right forefinger off the side of the frame and onto the trigger. The gun is already cocked. Burelle tilts her head to the right and looks down the sight. "It's over, Fulton. Your crap ends here."

"Don't Burelle. He's not armed, and you'll be sent to prison. I'm a cop, and I can do this," says Esch.

Burelle's eyes narrow. She takes a steadying breath.

"Don't argue, bitches. It's cold out here. Somebody just pull the trigger," sneers Fulton.

"How about we all just settle back. Burelle, you put that gun down now." While he doesn't have his weapon drawn, Chief Russo's holster is unsnapped. "Fulton, you just walk this way. Don't say anything; just come and get in my car. I'm not here to listen to any nonsense. We've all had a tough day, and we're a bit edgy." Esch steps forward, places her hand on Burelle's right forearm, and gently pushes it down.

Fulton walks past the burly man to where a deputy stands with his revolver drawn and a pair of handcuffs. "I was only kidding, Chief. Can't anyone take a joke anymore? I wasn't able to get to take my son out for Halloween and got to feeling sorry for myself and maybe had one too many. Jesus Christ, I'm sorry, but I meant no harm."

"Get in the car, Fulton. I'll let you sleep it off at the jail, and we'll talk in the morning." When Fulton is locked in the back seat of the chief's car, Russo walks inside to speak with Burelle and Esch. He finds Hogan sitting at the kitchen table wiping blood off his face. "Do you want to press charges, Hogan?"

"Fuck. He's my son. What will he get? A slap on the wrist? The judge'll say he just wanted to see Randy, and I let him in, which I did." Hogan shakes his head.

Russo turns to Burelle and Esch. "What about you guys?"

"What for? Making my girls cry?" asks Esch. She sits with her girls on the couch, one on each thigh. Both are sucking their thumbs, mirror images of one another.

"Where's Random?" asks Russo.

"He's been through this drill before at Morvid's house. He knows to hide when his dad shows up drunk." Burelle's shoulders slump. "We know he'll be back out after a day or two; he always is. He'll say he's sorry, that he was upset over not being able to see his son, that they bought matching costumes, that he won't do it again. Morvid will tell the judge that he'll see to it that Fulton stays sober. He'll tell the judge Fulton deserves a break as a Vietnam vet. He'll say

Fulton struggles because his father and mother deserted him, and the judge will concur. Who wants to put the unemployed Vietnam vet from the family of the town's leading retired banker in jail?" Burelle purses her lips and turns to see Random at the top of the stairs. She smiles and nods, a sign that the coast is clear. Random bounds down the stairs and into his mother's arms. Without turning to the police chief, she answers his first question. "If you can put him away for a long time, then I'll press charges. If you can't, then I won't. A short stay will just piss him off more."

§

Chief Russo books Fulton into the city jail. Hogan refuses any medical help, except for what Burelle and Esch provide, and then he goes to Random's room to sit with his grandson. Burelle and Esch need to unwind. The two women stay up early into the morning talking about Burelle's near future. The gentility of Esch's voice flows into Burelle's soul. It always has. The twins sleep on the couch, and Burelle fixes tea. Rather than sit at the kitchen table, the two women sit on the floor near Esch's children and try to unwind. Eventually, Esch steers the conversation to dating.

"It's a reward I give myself. I let Joey pamper me, and I flirt. It's fun, and we're not serious yet."

"I wouldn't know how. I've never had a date." Burelle's statement stuns Esch. "You knew that, didn't you?"

"Never?" replies Esch. "In all this time, it never registered. So, except for Fulton, you're a virgin." Esch knows immediately that her mouth has gotten ahead of her. She reaches over and touches Burelle's forearm. "I'm sorry. I didn't mean it like that."

"It's okay."

They sit quietly for a moment and sip their tea. Then Esch speaks again. "I have a guy for you. He's a little older and a teacher at the elementary school. Tom Renfroe. Joey introduced me to him, and I told him about you. He'd like to ask you out. He's cute, Burelle, and nice."

Burelle looks over to Esch. "If we went out and he touched me, I'd probably flinch so suddenly that I'd scare him away. He'd think

I'm some kind of weirdo or something." She smiles, the first one of the late evening. "Esch, dear, I've never had a man touch me in a suggestive way. I've never kissed a man. My only contact with that was" and here Burelle pauses. She curls her lips inward between her teeth and sniffles. "My only contact is . . . camping."

Esch rolls onto her knees and moves in front of Burelle. She looks into Burelle's eyes for several moments, tilting her head as if she's a doctor examining a patient. Burelle sits still and waits. In time, Esch raises her hand to Burelle's face. With her forefinger she traces the outline of Burelle's chin, moves it gently across her cheeks and under her nose, then up the bridge of her nose and over Burelle's eyebrows. Esch pulls her hand back in order to slide closer into Burelle's body. Esch reaches out and hugs her friend tightly. She doesn't loosen her hold when Burelle stays motionless; instead, Esch turns her face into Burelle's neck and kisses it. Burelle leans into Esch's lips and breathes deeply. It's a sensation she has never experienced, and it feels good. She raises her left arm and places it around Esch's shoulders, trying not to allow Esch's lips to leave her skin. In her entire life, Burelle's only experience with skin to skin intimacy has been with Random: mother to child.

Esch whispers into Burelle's ear, "Are you okay?"

"Uh-huh, I am."

"What else do you want me to do?"

"Just hold me and keep your lips on my neck." Burelle thinks about her words. There is something else. "No, I want you to kiss me too. Is that all right?"

Esch flicks her tongue on Burelle's neck before pulling back. "Close your eyes," she says. Esch puts her finger on Burelle's lips before moving to kiss her. It's gentle, the way a shy man might kiss a shy girl on her porch after their first movie. It does not suggest a move toward overt sex, only a touch meant to convey understanding in the deepest way. Esch keeps her lips on Burelle's for a minute before pulling back. Then she moves up and kisses both closed eyes tenderly.

"You can open your eyes now," Esch says.

Burelle smiles before she speaks. "Maybe I never will. That was wonderful." She opens them, however, and removes her arm from

Esch's shoulder.

"It's better with a man," says Esch.

"Then you'd better find me one soon."

Esch lies down with her head in Burelle's lap, and Burelle runs her fingers through Esch's hair.

"Could you have shot him?" asks Esch.

"Yes. I started to pull the trigger when I stepped by you, but I thought of Random. I'm not a Tree, but he is, sort of."

"You sure scared Fulton though."

"Maybe for an instant, but then he saw it in my eyes that I wasn't going to. He mocked me."

Esch laughs. "If you would have pulled the trigger on that gun, the recoil would have knocked you on your sweet ass. Your elbows were locked and too high."

Burelle gently tugs Esch's hair. "I've never shot a gun before. No dad around to teach me, but I've been holding Hogan's while everyone was out, learning to hold it properly. When did you learn?"

"I'm embarrassed to say. Fulton used to take me to shoot squirrels and birds out at the cabin. I was a better shot than him from the start, and it was another thing that pissed him off. When I went to school to be a cop, I spent lots of time on the range."

Burelle doesn't respond for a time. She sips her tea and looks across the room. Esch shifts around and scoots over to her girls. She brushes their hair and kisses each one on the forehead, leaving Burelle to her thoughts.

Burelle listens to the wind, a sound she hasn't been aware of since she stood at the window and watched the storm arrive several hours earlier. It doesn't sound like the wind to her, but like a river; a river's song calling her to board a dory and travel out to sea.

"Do you need some sleep, Burelle?"

"Yes."

"Quite a night, huh."

"Yes."

§

The next day, November 1, Hogan drives Burelle and Random

to Denver for passport photos. Random wears his Chewbacca costume and gets to miss a half-day of school. Hogan is unusually quiet, and Burelle senses why.

"It's not your fault, Hogan. You were hit by the door." She waits while Hogan searches for a response. "Anyway, we're all okay, and this will pass." She doesn't fully believe her own words.

Finally, Hogan speaks. "I sort of promised you that I'd protect you and Random, and I didn't last night." Burelle starts to interrupt, but Hogan cuts her off. "No. No, I didn't. That's the bottom line. I've got to get him into the Institute; he's just so unpredictable." Hogan leans toward Burelle's ear and whispers, "I'm afraid of him too. I think I always have been. I think it showed last night."

"What's the Institute, Grampa?" asks Random from the back seat.

"It's a place where your daddy might get some help in controlling his temper, a place where they might find out why he gets so angry at times."

"Oh," says Random. "That would be a good thing."

CHAPTER 25

Fulton spends three days in jail while Chief Russo maneuvers to satisfy everyone concerned and make his town safer. In the end misdemeanor charges are filed, Fulton apologizes to the judge at his hearing, and he's released with probation and a stern admonition to behave and find a steady job. Burelle reluctantly drops Random off at Morvid's on Saturday so Fulton can take him for a day of bonding. Compromise and bridge building; the judge's idea. Morvid purchases an undersized basketball for Random and installs a hoop in the den. The furniture has been moved to the opposite wall and the area rug rolled up to expose the hardwood floor. In the old Victorian room with its high ceilings, the basket measures seven feet high; Random dribbles the ball and shoots, letting great-grandpa Morvid rebound. Random, despite being small for his age, seems to have inherited his father's athletic ability, and he makes baskets frequently. Eagle Canyon's recreation department begins its "Junior Miners" basketball league at the third grade level.

"Where did you learn to shoot like that?" asked Morvid.

"Coach Whitehead. He's the coach at the high school, but he's my gym teacher. It's what we mostly do in gym class." Random had not wanted to go to Morvid's house, but his mother and Hogan assured him it would be okay. They will pick him up after supper.

"Your daddy was a good player back when he was in high school. Maybe he can teach you some things about the game too." Morvid bounces a pass to Random and moves back to the basket.

"When's he going to be here?"

"Any time now. He said he had to finish up plowing some snow for a friend and then he'd be here. He's anxious to spend some time with you. He'll like how you shoot."

Random continues to shoot for the better part of an hour. At noon Morvid makes a couple of phone calls. Then he returns to the den. "Why don't we go get a couple of burgers for lunch while we wait for your daddy. We can come back here and watch some football on TV. He shouldn't be too much longer." Morvid and Random bundle up and walk three blocks to the Burger Barn and then return to have lunch on TV trays while they watch the Sooners play the Cowboys. Morvid listens as Random explains the football plays occurring on the screen. Morvid knows football, but he asks questions and listens intently to Random. The little boy takes the Sooners' side and assigns Morvid the Cowboys. As the game progresses, the oohs and aahs increase. Random's Sooners pull away, and Random is free to tease his great grandpa about the outcome. The little boy forgets about the absence of his father to the point that Morvid hopes Fulton won't arrive, hopes that this afternoon can be the beginning of a better relationship for the oldest Tree and the youngest.

At five o'clock, Morvid makes another call. "So you haven't heard from him all day?" Morvid hangs up and calls Hogan. "Yeah, he got delayed at work and won't be home tonight, so I'll drive Random over."

§

It's Burelle's twenty-fourth birthday on this Saturday, but she hasn't told anyone. After leaving Random at Morvid's, she goes to work, choosing to build up extra hours of overtime to accumulate a small nest egg, a savings account for the journey. She once had one from the sale of her trailer, but that money is long gone. It was very little to begin with. She re-opened the account when she began working at the police department, and she already has nearly one hundred dollars.

The day is quiet at work. Last week's snowfall, over a foot, has muted the town's activities on the side streets, although the businesses just off the interstate are gearing up for the ski season. Only the oldest deputy and the dispatcher are at the office, and Burelle is able to get cleaning tasks completed that normally would be delayed. She spends four hours in Chief Russo's office without interruption, working through lunch. He won't notice, or if he does, he won't say much, but she's proud of her work. Burelle has a vague memory of sitting in the chief's office many years ago while her mother filled out papers. Burelle was about Random's age then, and the visit was about her father's repeated attacks on his mother. After that visit she never saw her father again.

In the time since she moved in with Hogan, Burelle has restyled her hair and begun to wear eyeshadow, both at Esch's insistence. Esch makes no secret about wanting to get Burelle a boyfriend and jokes about getting her laid. Burelle laughs, but the thought both intrigues and frightens her. Tonight will be the first step; she will meet Esch's choice and double date with Esch and her current boyfriend, Joey Sessions, for pizza and a movie. Tom Renfroe teaches at the elementary school, fifth grade. He has no connections to Eagle Canyon from his past, and he's a nice man, according to Esch. Blind dates appear from the oddest places, and this one is no different. Tom teaches Joey's son, who wandered off over the summer and got lost in the foothills above Eagle Canyon, and Officer Esch found him during the search. Tom helped in the search, and it was he who walked Esch and the boy back down the trail to Joey. Tom stands six-foot-five, "tall enough for you," and has dimples deep enough to crawl into, so Esch made the plans. Fulton's Halloween tirade and the intimate talk that night pushed Esch toward a quicker date for Burelle.

Burelle returns from work to several surprises. Random is home and he and Hogan have a store-bought cake waiting for her along with a card and a small present. Her choice would be to stay home and enjoy Random, but the date with Tom can't be postponed. "Open it!" insists Random. It is a stuffed animal, an unidentified creature, until Random discloses that it's a Wookiee.

§

Eagle Canyon's movie theater has only a single screen, so there is no discussion over which movie everyone wants. Viewers watch what is being shown. To get a choice, the town's residents must drive to Denver. Tonight, the film is "Close Encounters of the Third Kind." Dinner will be pizza afterwards. Esch has decided to make Burelle's first date as casual and comfortable as possible, and she models "dating protocol" with Joey as much as possible. He was prepped on the situation earlier and understands his role. No kissing, no arm around the shoulder in the movie, open car doors, hold the chair at dinner as Esch sits down, don't concentrate on his own date, but draw Tom and Burelle into the conversation. In other words, make it a friends gathering rather than strictly a date.

Tom needs no prepping. He seems eager just to get to know Burelle. He walks beside her but does not hold her hand. He places his hand in the small of her back to guide her to a seat in the theater and pizza parlor, and he touches her forearm to get her attention at the table. Everyone laughs and Tom plays the stereotypical big guy who puts people at ease. "I kept getting hungry when Richard Dreyfus swirled his mashed potatoes. It seemed like such a waste of good food. Then again, I kind of like any movie that has food in it." Burelle laughs.

She watches Tom. She notices the crooked ring finger on his right hand, his habit of biting the right side of his lower lip while he listens to others, his absolute politeness with the restaurant servers, and that every little kid at both the theater and the pizza parlor seems to know him. "How long have you taught here in town?" she asks.

"This is my fifth year. I taught four years before this down in the San Luis Valley. This is nicer. Before that I was a soldier in Vietnam." Burelle tenses momentarily. "I got out and put that nonsense behind me. No sense in bringing it up all the time."

"I'm twenty-five. How old are you?" Burelle asks.

Tom laughs. "Thirty-three, but people say I still behave like a teenager sometimes."

"Those are years I don't want to repeat." She pauses. "I've lived here my whole life. Can you tell?"

Esch and Joey shift in their seats at Burelle's questions, but Tom doesn't flinch. He uses both hands to rub the sides of his nose before responding. "I didn't think there were any natives of Eagle Canyon over the age of eighteen. All my colleagues are from somewhere else, and I live in the new apartments on the east end of town. No one who lives there is a native." He reaches over and squeezes Burelle's shoulder and allows his hand to linger. "I'm kidding a little. Every small town has its natives, but I seldom interact with them at school. When I'm teaching at school, it's just me and my students, and nobody interferes with us, not even the natives." Burelle reaches up and touches Tom's hand but says nothing. Joey looks at his watch and nudges Esch.

Fifteen minutes later Tom escorts Burelle to her door, places his hands on the tops of her shoulders, and kisses her goodnight on the cheek.

"Tell me, was I okay?" she asks.

Tom's hands transmit her subtle shudder into his chest. He has responded to this type of question from so many of his fifth-grade students, so he knows its importance. Am I okay? He tilts his head, uses his index finger to lift her chin slightly in order to gain her eyes. "That's the question I was about to ask you. You were so okay that I want to see you again, but I was afraid you thought maybe I'm too goofy." He holds her with his eyes. "You were wonderful, Burelle, and I had a really good time."

Burelle smiles and nods, mostly to herself. A moment later she rises up on her toes and kisses Tom lightly on his lips, holding his lips like Esch taught her on Halloween. "Okay, then. Call me in the morning."

As she turns to go inside, Random taps on the window and waves, then pulls the curtain shut like he's playing hide-and-go-seek.

"Randy's a bit of a star at school, you know. He's handled this whole affair quite well; he doesn't seem to be struggling with it like the other two boys do. You've taken care of him in the right way."

§

Tom calls on Sunday morning, and Burelle invites him to join her, Random, and Hogan for a morning of tubing on the crowded hill near the park where Eagle Canyon families gather to picnic in the summer. During the winter months, when there is adequate snow, the hill teems with teens and younger children of the town, and the rare parent who dares the steep slope. Burelle and Esch tubed the slope when they were young, but it has been years since she last put her butt in a tube and slid down.

Random has no fear. He gets a running start at the top of the hill and jumps onto his tube belly first. Hogan catches him at the bottom and carries the tube over to the rope tow so that Random can go again. Burelle and Tom stand together to allow grandpa his time with Randy. Just like the evening before, many of the kids on the hill come over to Mr. Renfroe to say hi. After several runs Random challenges Tom to take a run down the hill with him, and Tom accepts the challenge. He borrows the largest inner tube he sees on the hill, one still too small for his large frame, and joins Random at the top. Hogan and Burelle wait at the bottom.

Tom rides like Random does, belly down and face first. Near the bottom of the hill, Tom hits a mogul and is thrown out in a heap. Burelle covers her mouth with both hands and awaits the outcome. Tom plays the accident for all it's worth before standing and bowing, drawing a round of applause from the other tubers. Random makes several more runs with his friends as Tom recounts his one run with Burelle and Hogan while they sit at a picnic bench watching the tubers and sledders. Random eventually tires out and joins them at the table.

"I've never met a family with so many unique names," says Tom. My brothers are John and Bob. My sister is Mary, and my parents are Robert and Alice." Tom helps Random up onto the tabletop to sit.

"You're tall," says Random.

"Yep. I'm the tallest one in my family. It helps when I need to reach things on shelves, but it's not so good when I try to fit in a tube to slide down the hill. Makes me look clumsy."

"My daddy's tall, but not as tall as you," says Random. Burelle tenses, cringes really, just as she always does when Fulton's name is mentioned.

Either Tom had been warned by Esch or he has the sense not to go there, and he allows Random's remark to pass. Shortly thereafter, he stands to excuse himself. "I've enjoyed meeting you Mr. Tree." Tom turns to Random and bends down to shake his hand. "I'll be seeing you at school. Maybe in a few years, you'll be in my class."

Burelle takes Tom's hand and walks him to his car. Hogan grabs Random's inner tube, and they walk to the rope tow.

CHAPTER 26

A minor traffic ticket sets Fulton off again. Blind rage. Morvid can't calm him down but does convince him to drive out to the cabin and let off steam. Shoot up some trees. It hasn't snowed since the big one in late October, on Halloween night, so the road to the lake is once again open. Fulton scares Morvid with his talk of getting even, with his threat to get that son-of-a-bitch police officer who wrote the ticket. Fifteen miles over the limit in the school zone. For Christ's sake, school has been out for nearly two hours. Morvid wants to call Chief Russo, but knows that will only make Fulton angrier, knows the chief can't do anything more than talk to Fulton. Morvid fears that if he does anything, Fulton will beat him again. Finally, after Fulton leaves, Morvid calls the one person Fulton seems to fear.

"Son, I hate to bother you, but Fulton's gone crazy again, and I'm afraid he might do something stupid."

Hogan and Random are just finishing the dishes when the phone rings. Burelle and Tom sit in the living room watching TV after a stay-at-home dinner date. Since it's Wednesday, Tom promised not to stay long. All the adults have work in the morning, and Random has school. Hogan lifts Random from the metal stool where he stands to put the glasses away and sends him to go sit with his mom and Tom.

"Fulton's always crazy and always angry. I've warned you over and over that he needs to be locked up. You need to press charges so there's a police record." Hogan catches himself and asks, "What happened this time? Did he hit you?"

"No, but I thought he might. He got a speeding ticket and the officer lectured him on the spot. He drove over to the police station and demanded Captain Green tear it up. I guess he got pretty loud, and they threatened to lock him up if he didn't leave. Broke a few things over here, so I sent him out to the cabin."

"Shit, Morvid, he just drinks and stews out there."

"I didn't know what else to do. He just seems to be having a bad spell these days. He can't find work so easy when winter comes."

Hogan pulls the phone from his ear and rubs it against his head. He breathes out heavily. "Do you know for sure that he went to the cabin?"

"No, but he usually does when he gets angry, and he can sleep off the booze."

"I want you to go down to the police office and stay there. Tell them what you just told me. No matter what, you stay there. Get out of the house until I come and get you."

"Are you gonna go get him?"

"Just go. I'll do what I can." Hogan hangs up the phone and turns his back to the wall to think. He remembers why Gertie left. He picks up the phone and calls the police office. "Can I talk to Chief Russo please?" When he finishes speaking with Russo, Hogan makes a second call to the West Denver Institute. "He needs to be there! What if I got him restrained and brought him in? He scares people around here. He's going to hurt someone one of these days. You helped me, and he needs your help more than I did." He hangs up the phone tensely. All the letters and phone calls, but the Institute moves slowly, cautiously. They suggest the Veterans Administration for immediate help. They've agreed to an evaluation, but there are conditions. Since Fulton is an adult, the Institute wants him to commit himself. Hogan composes himself and goes into the living room. Random sits between Burelle and Tom.

Burelle speaks first. "Did you send Random in here to chaperone?"

"Do you need one?" replies Hogan.

"Are you okay? Who was on the phone?"

Because of Burelle's history of abuse from Fulton, Hogan never hides the dangers from her. "Morvid called. Fulton's having one of his meltdowns tonight and wants me to go find him. I don't want you and Random here alone though."

Tom knows a little about Burelle's situation, but not about the abuse. "How about if I stay here while you go find him?"

Hogan rubs his forehead. "I was thinking maybe you could take them over to your place for a while. Until I get a handle on this."

After bundling up Random and packing his toothbrush, Burelle puts him in Tom's car to head out for his apartment. She hugs Hogan for comfort and tells him to be careful. He orders her to stay with Tom until he calls. He shakes hands with Tom and tells him that it's probably nothing, but to be alert. Tom seems to understand the severity of the situation. Then, Hogan returns to the house to get his pistol. In the dark a truck follows Tom's car.

§

Fulton drives to The Jungle rather than up to the cabin. He starts drinking with two of his bar buddies and unloads his story. Hogan and Chief Russo spot his car parked on the side street across from the bar around midnight after they have driven up to the cabin and found nothing. Wednesday nights in Eagle Canyon in early winter do not bring out big crowds to The Jungle, so Fulton's rants don't create much of a stir. Russo and Hogan stay in the chief's cruiser and observe.

"I don't know whether to close up The Jungle or make sure it stays open, whether it encourages our town's jerks or gives them an outlet," says the police chief.

"Probably a little of both. Just after high school, if I recall, we both spent a little bit of time there," replies Hogan.

"What a name. The Jungle." Russo considers the culture at the bar, thinks about those who frequent this tavern. "This may be the only place in town where Fulton feels welcome, and it's even iffy here."

"We may have dodged a bullet tonight, Roos. Morvid said Fulton was pretty angry."

Russo nods. "He seems to be getter angrier and angrier by the week. Was he an angry kid growing up, Hogan, or is this a post-war thing?"

"When he was real young, when he was a boy, he seemed to get real pleasure in hurting animals and my wife. I got rid of two dogs and a cat because he mistreated them. I had to put the cat down. With Gertie, it was just a nastiness. She tried to love him, but he was . . . unlovable." Hogan searches for another word. "Maybe detached and manipulative. Only when I would back him into a corner did he ever concede anything or apologize." He pauses again, and the chief waits, allowing Hogan the choice to reveal more about his son. "He broke Gertie's arm and dislocated her shoulder. Only twelve-years-old. The doctor suspected me, the crazy man, not Fulton. That's when I sent her away."

"It must have been hard for you." Russo waits for an answer, but Hogan stays silent. "I know you've been looking for a place to put him, a hospital or something, but I wonder, would he ever go willingly?"

"No. The place I was at keeps saying they'll give him an evaluation someday, but they keep postponing it. Judge Quinn said I'd need some specific evidence for him to intervene, but Fulton and Morvid stay just behind the line. Fulton's an unfeeling man."

Russo nods ever so slightly, and both men are quiet. "Even if we could get him in, do you think he's beyond treatment?"

"The Institute helped me, but mine was depression . . . and guilt. Fulton's way past that. I'd like to think he could be fixed, but more and more, I just don't know."

Just after one-fifteen, Fulton emerges with a middle-aged woman and leaves in her car. Russo and Hogan follow them to an old Victorian rooming house in west Eagle Canyon where Main Street flows into the interstate. Fulton and the woman help each other inside.

Back at the police station, Hogan calls Burelle. Tom answers. "That's good news, I guess. Burelle's asleep in my bed with Random. I won the couch in the coin flip. I'll see them home in the morning. No sense in taking them home tonight. One of these days, I'd like for you to tell me what I'm getting into. Maybe Burelle shouldn't tell me just yet." Hogan promises he will. He likes Tom Renfroe and thinks he's good for Burelle.

Chief Russo calls his deputy on his car radio and tells him he can end the surveillance, go home, and get some sleep. As Hogan turns to leave, Russo shakes his hand. "Thanks for the heads-up tonight. I'll talk with Judge Quinn tomorrow."

Morvid has fallen asleep in one of the two holding cells, ignoring what's happening outside. He and Captain Green stayed up talking about Fulton. The captain mostly listened to the old man. All of Eagle Canyon's law enforcement employees have had dealings with Fulton, and each time, Morvid has tried to explain. Tonight is no exception. There is no convincing Morvid that his grandson is a sick person; Morvid will have none of that.

§

Tom Renfroe quietly enters his bedroom to check on his new girlfriend. The light from the hallway casts a soft hue on Burelle, and Tom studies her features. When Esch was setting him up with Burelle, she told him that Burelle wasn't pretty, but was above average. Tom disagrees. Jet black hair, brown eyes, and a beautiful smile—when she smiles, which has been much more forthcoming as they spend time together. She likes him, and she listens to him, making Tom believe he's important and interesting. It's early in their relationship, but there's something special already. Tom has always been comfortable about himself, and it's obvious to him that Burelle lacks that confidence. Still, even in their very short time together, Burelle's tenseness has dissipated. She likes hugging, and her body melds into his.

From under the covers, Burelle extends her hand. "Don't stand there and gawk. Take off your shoes and lay next to me. I trust you."

§

On Thursday morning Fulton returns to the police station to seek out the officer who wrote the speeding ticket. Fulton apologizes for his attitude of the previous day, even going so far as to compare his behavior with a spoiled teenager. He offers his hand and promises to behave. "It won't happen again." When he leaves, the young officer goes in to speak with Captain Green to get his take on what had just happened.

"Charming fellow when he wants to be," replies the captain. "Don't turn your back on him."

§

At the local river park on Saturday morning, Tom sits with Burelle on a picnic bench and gives her his first present. A single, smooth, yellow stone hangs from a black leather string. "I showed it to Hogan yesterday, and he said it reminds him of a thing he does for good luck, something about smooth stones being returned to the river. It didn't quite make sense, but I hope you like it."

CHAPTER 27

Burelle and Tom stroll the bike lane in silence. The hum of cars from the interstate across the valley can be heard, but neither minds. Three days earlier, they had lain together in his bed, one in pajamas and one fully dressed except for shoes. Big Tom had put his arm around Burelle as if to protect her, and he felt the movements of her body: a heartbeat, small spasms, large shudders, irregular breathing patterns. He understands. In Vietnam, when he held wounded soldiers, he felt the same thing. Today, he holds her gloved hand with his bare hand. Cold weather never seems to affect him.

Burelle watches the light play against the mountain cliffs on this partly cloudy afternoon. Ice has formed on the banks of the river, and each day it edges closer to covering the entire flow. This is Hogan's path, although he avoids it in winter. Unlike Tom, Hogan feels the cold and doesn't like it. He's more comfortable in the school's boiler room. Burelle intentionally bumps her shoulder into Tom's arm as they walk. They smile at each other but say little. It's a comfortable silence. Last night, they drove to Denver for dinner and a movie, and when they came back to Eagle Canyon, they made love.

Tom worries it's too soon, that Burelle will think it's what he wants above anything else. She would be wrong. He didn't plan on it, but the kissing pushed buttons on Burelle that once depressed could not be reversed. Tom doesn't have much experience with sex; some, but not a lot. As he walks, he wonders what she is thinking, but he is not about to ask yet.

Burelle would tell him. It was wonderful. It was a gift. It was unbelievable. I'm glad it was you. Can we make love again tonight?

Please. She releases his hand and steps in front of him, making him stop. His eyes ask, What? Her face smiles up at him, and then she steps into his body and hugs him. When the hug ends, Burelle asks, "Are you planning to teach in Eagle Canyon for the rest of your life?"

"Hmm." They turn and start back toward town, and Tom takes Burelle's hand again. "Yeah, I could do that, but I wouldn't have to. This is a nice district and a nice little town. The people are good, and parents care about their kids getting a good education." He smiles gently to himself, thinking he knows where this is going. "As long as I could get another teaching job elsewhere, I wouldn't need to stay here. It's what I do. It's what I am. But if you're worried about Fulton, I can take care of you."

"Hogan says you're really good at teaching, and he knows. He wanted to be a teacher once, but he says he was afraid to get in front of all those kids. He observes all the teachers, though, and he respects you."

"Hogan wanted to teach? That surprises me."

Burelle squeezes Tom's hand. "He went to college before his war to get a degree in teaching, but he got wounded and lost some hearing and never finished. I think he regrets it sometimes. He loves being around you teachers and all the students."

Tom returns to Burelle's earlier question. "Are you planning on leaving Eagle Canyon?"

Burelle looks straight ahead. She remembers Hogan's warning. "Someday. Sooner than later, I hope. You know why."

This woman has tornadoes in her soul, thinks Tom. Even though they have been together for such a short time, he believes they are meant for one another. He called his parents and told them about her and Random, and he told his sister. They want to meet Burelle, and he wants her to meet them. "Would your plans allow me to finish the school year?"

"If they didn't, if I left sooner, would you follow me? Would you come and get me, even if I went half-way around the world?"

On the edge of town, a car slows allowing a young boy to stick his head out of the window. "Hey, Mr. Renfroe." Tom waves and they continue to walk while Tom considers his answer. "You aren't the only one who has plans, Burelle. After our first week together, I sat down and wrote down a path for us. Last night occurred a lot earlier than my plan. I wanted to go slow so you could get to know me, know that I'm a pretty nice guy, naïve, but nice. I want you to know that if we get together, it would be forever. Excuse me for being blunt, but I know you think that you have some baggage, but I don't see it, and I don't care. You are what you are now."

Burelle looks down, then leans over and bumps Tom's arm again. "Having a hard time answering my question, huh?" She keeps her head down, smiling. She knows.

"Yeah, Miss Oakley. I'd come for you."

CHAPTER 28

"Who was that on the phone, sweetheart?" asks Burelle. She sets her hair dryer on the kitchen counter freeing her hands to pour Random a glass of juice.

"Dad. He wants me to stay home from school this morning. He said he'd come by and take me to breakfast, and then drop me off at school later." Random squinches up his nose, an indication he'd rather not. "We're practicing our Christmas play this morning. It's Friday night."

"I know. Just finish your breakfast, and I'll let him know you can't miss school today." She doesn't feel it will be necessary, since Fulton probably won't show up anyway, and she won't leave Random alone at home waiting. Still, she will leave a note on the door telling him that breakfast with his son will have to wait until the weekend.

Burelle likes the morning routine. Hogan wakes first. His routine has been altered since she and Random moved in, but it's obvious he's happy about it. They haven't discussed their secret, but they share a smile about it each day. He won't tell her when, but she senses it's getting closer. He's kidded Random about a Christmas plane ride. At first, her new relationship with Tom Renfroe caused her some concern, but that's not a problem. Hogan always has toast, orange juice, and a banana. He gets his coffee at school, his own brew in the custodian's office, and he drinks several cups while he works. He stays at the house just long enough to say good morning to Burelle before she showers. If snow has fallen overnight, he will have it all shoveled except for the short stretch from the porch to the sidewalk. That's Random's morning chore, something Hogan believes is important for a boy to learn, something to get his body in motion before heading off to his "real job." Most mornings there is no snow, so his job is to exercise Tinker in the back yard. Random isn't up when Hogan leaves; the two of them will meet before school just inside the southwest doors where most of the kids enter the building and close to his classroom. Burelle fixes breakfast, either a hot cereal or eggs and bacon. They eat together, although like this morning she usually stands and cleans while Random sits, and then he will walk to school with two classmates, Noah and Jack. Burelle follows a comfortable distance behind, passes by the school where she can wave to Tom when he has bus duty, and head to the police station another block down. Routines. Burelle likes this one.

"Get your gloves and stocking hat. It's too cold for a baseball cap."

Random tosses his cap back into the wicker basket by the door. He has already forgotten about his dad's call. He stuffs his lunch sack into his gym bag for basketball practice after school and watches out the window for his friends.

§

Esch's parents are Eagle Canyon natives. Esch's mother babysits the girls when Esch has early patrol. Grandpa Esch manages the Joslin's clothing store, what was once the old Crews-Beggs Mercantile. Wednesday mornings are her scheduled day at Whitman Elementary, the day when she talks to individual classes, addresses special concerns, walks the hallways, and generally makes her presence felt to the students. There are other days when she will be at Whitman, but she always "serves and protects" on Wednesdays. Police work has its routines, and these often get upset by a pressing need, but for Officer Esch, Wednesdays remain a joyful constant. She broke up with Joey and has been flirting with one of Tom's colleagues, an art teacher who pretends to be a beatnik.

§

Tom Renfroe arrives early to school, one of the handful of teachers who shows up an hour before the opening bell. Still, he seldom beats Hogan to work, who is often the first staff member at school.

On this day Hogan has sidewalks to shovel, a persnickety boiler to attend to, and a bank of lights in the gym that mysteriously has gone out. Often over the last month, Tom has joined Hogan in the custodian's office for a quick chat and a cup of coffee, and he has come in this morning. Hogan believes Tom could create a stable family condition for Burelle and Randy, and because of this, Hogan has delayed the trip. He wants Burelle to be happy too.

"Morning, Hogan. Coldest day of the year so far, and wouldn't you know it, I have bus duty."

"How were the roads driving in?" asks Hogan.

"Good. Not enough snow to pack, and the cold didn't allow any of it to melt and then refreeze into ice. I don't know what it's like on the interstate though. Coffee ready yet?"

"Yeah." Hogan hands Tom a mug. "How did you get Randy to stop laughing last night?"

"I couldn't. It was Burelle. Once I started my armpit farting, he just couldn't stop. I'm not sure Burelle thought it was so funny though."

Hogan wants to ask Tom if he would be open to leaving America and living in New Zealand, but he doesn't know how to broach the subject. It's a discussion he will have though. They talk only for a few more minutes before Tom needs to leave to xerox a worksheet before heading out to the playground where the buses let off the kids. Also, he wants to wave at Burelle when she passes by on her way to work. Hogan will work his way around to the door where Random's room is located so he can say hi and muss his hair.

§

Halfway to work, about a block from school, Burelle remembers that she didn't leave the note for Fulton. She considers ignoring it since going back will mean she will most likely miss seeing Tom, but she told Random she would, so she turns and heads back to the house. If she hurries, maybe Tom will still be out on bus duty. The cold is biting, and she covers her ears with her mittens. Grab a hat on the way out, Burelle, she tells herself. Her note is brief; Random has practice for the Christmas pageant in the morning and can't miss it; Fulton can call and set up breakfast for the weekend if he'd like. There's more she'd like to say, like could he please give her a little more time before he wants Random, but she lets it go. Fulton won't change. She just hopes if he comes by, he doesn't get too angry, but she figures he will. Burelle grabs a woolen scarf, closes the door, wedges the note between the metal frame and the screen on the screen door at eye level, and starts walking back to the police station. If I hurry, she thinks, I may still get to see Tom.

§

Fulton is out of Morvid's house before seven, having coffee and a roll at the convenience store next to the new McDonald's. He didn't check on Morvid before he left; he just grabbed his duffle bag and headed out. On another day Morvid would have wanted to lecture him anyway, but not today. The last thing Morvid said last night was "Why can't we disagree without you getting angry and wanting to hit me?"

Fulton is startled when Chief Russo enters the convenience store. After buying a half-dozen doughnuts, Russo notices Fulton at the little table and nods. "The bakery didn't open this morning. Its pipes froze." Russo laughs. "A law officer has to have his breakfast, doesn't he?" The two men smile at each other. "Say hi to your pop for me."

Outside, Russo sits in his car and ponders Fulton. What would he be like if he had a permanent job? What would he be like if he moved out of his father's house and was forced to take responsibility for his own actions? Russo makes a note to call Judge Quinn again, and then heads back to the station with breakfast, but he thinks he missed an opportunity just now to be nice to Fulton. The chief wonders if anyone in town will really be nice to Fulton today. Four blocks down, Russo passes the construction site for a twelve-unit condominium. "Hiring." Russo makes a U-turn into the site, jots down the number, and then heads back to the convenience store.

CHAPTER 29

Fulton has left the convenience store by the time Chief Russo returns. Russo asks the clerk if Fulton said anything about where he was going, and the clerk recalls Fulton mentioning something about taking his son out for breakfast, about driving him to Denver where it's warmer and going to a park too. He's not sure. Back in his car, Russo backs onto the main drag, turns on his emergency flashing lights, and drives quickly toward the center of town, toward the elementary school. Russo remembers the last time Fulton wanted to see his boy and jerked him out of class. The police chief does not want a repeat of that incident.

§

The last school bus drops off its kids. It's the rural route bus, and its passengers have the longest ride each morning and afternoon, some as long as an hour. A dozen other students stay outside in the cold to throw puff balls or play tag, but most have already entered the building and shed their winter coats. Mr. Renfroe has a warm smile and a pat on the shoulder for these late arriving few as they step off the bus. He towers over these elementary students, like a giant among elves. Tom notices a lone man standing behind the bus as it pulls away. Something seems wrong. Even though it's cold, the man stands perfectly still and stares at the school. He wears a cowboy hat and duster, and a bandana covers his face, protecting it from the brisk wind. A bag hangs from one shoulder, while his hands are stuffed in his pockets. He steps off the curb and walks directly toward Tom, simultaneously pulling his bandana down with his left hand and an object out of his coat with his right. At that moment Tom recognizes both the man and the Browning 9mm pistol. Mr. Renfroe yells at the students to quickly run inside the building, that it's time for classes to begin, and he takes two steps in the direction of Fulton Tree to head him off.

The first shot strikes Tom in his hip, knocking him to the snowy playground. An instant later, a second round penetrates his chest and explodes his heart. Fulton continues to walk forward firing shots at anyone moving. He stops next to Tom's body. Four bullets ricochet off the school's wall, but finally a bullet hits a second grader in the jaw. Two more students are shot before they can enter the building: Maggie and Emily, six-year-old first graders who were holding hands when they got off the bus. Hearing the gunfire, the principal, Don Springston, runs from the building and surveys the scene. He sees four bodies lying on the ground, all with pools of blood staining the snow. Emily cries out, and the principal takes steps toward her, but he is shot in the leg by Fulton just as he gets to where she lays. Fulton fires the rest of his magazine without hitting anyone. He tosses the pistol aside, kneels to unzip his duffle bag, and removes another pistol, already loaded.

Officer Esch bursts out of the building and runs directly at Fulton. He raises his weapon, fires, and cuts her down with a single shot to the chest. Her momentum rolls her forward slightly, and Fulton shoots her once more in the back while she lies on the ground. Sounds from behind a concrete pillar near the door attract Fulton's attention. Students are screaming at what they are witnessing. A boy steps from behind the pillar toward the fallen officer and stares directly at Fulton.

Fulton turns slightly and aims his pistol at the boy but hesitates momentarily. "You're not supposed to be here. I'm going to take you to breakfast after this is over."

Random Tree doesn't move. His eyes remain glued to his father's eyes. Finally, he speaks. "I don't understand."

Burelle hears the gunfire from two blocks away and knows instantly what is happening. She screams, a guttural sound emanating from deep inside her chest. She runs a half-block before she slips and falls. She rises, leaving her purse in the snow, and runs again toward the death sounds. As she rounds the corner, she sees Random standing over a body in a police uniform. She also sees a man pointing a gun at her son. She stops. Every atom in her body stops moving; she is paralyzed and silent. There is no oxygen in her lungs.

One more adult bursts out of the school door hoping to shield Random. Fulton notices Hogan but jerks his attention back to Random and pulls the trigger. At that same moment, a second shot hits Fulton in the head, killing him instantly.

CHAPTER 30

For a moment there is no sound on the school playground. The echo of two simultaneous gunshots is silence, as if they exploded next to every person's ears and left them all deaf. And then, in slow motion still bodies find life. Hogan moves toward his grandson who lies draped over Officer Esch. Don Springston lifts himself onto his elbow and puts his other arm around Emily. Police Chief Russo lowers his rifle and yells for everyone who is able to move into the school building. Seven students stand from behind the pillar and scurry into the school. Ten people remain near the school's entrance: four students and six adults.

Chief Russo moves quickly to Fulton and kicks the pistol away from his body, bends over him and places his fingers along Fulton's neck to check for a pulse. Russo says something under his breath that no one can hear and then drops his head momentarily. He swivels his big body and moves instinctively to the boy with the facial wound. Noah Samuels. The chief lays his rifle on the ground and takes his handkerchief from his coat pocket. He gently lifts Noah's head and wraps the cloth around the boy's jaw and neck. Even though the boy is unconscious, Russo talks to him. "I've got you, son. You're going to be okay. Hang in there with me." Shopkeepers, neighbors, parents, and additional law enforcement personal begin to appear. Two women approach Burelle and place a blanket over her shoulders. All three begin walking toward the school. A station wagon speeds up to the playground with a doctor and four nurses. Coats are thrown over the bodies of Tom Renfroe, Grace Esch, Emily Gordon, Maggie Williams, and Fulton Tree. Reverend Chamberlain and other ministers and priests from the town kneel beside each body and pray. A light snow begins to fall, crystalline-like. The doctor and two nurses work to stabilize Noah Samuels, while two other nurses bandage the principal's leg. Russo stands, picking up his rifle as he rises. He hands it to Sergeant Collins and asks, "Esch?" The officer shakes his head. Russo surveys the playground, pausing momentarily at each body. He turns back to the sergeant. "I'm going to need you to go get Morvid. Take the old fool down to the station and lock him in a cell. Don't tell him anything. Then come back here. We've got plenty to do."

Random Tree is reluctant to move away from Officer Esch's body, but Hogan sits next to him on the snowy asphalt and pulls the little boy into his lap. A local merchant wraps a coat around both of them and remains standing over them. For the second time in four months, Random has survived a mass shooting unscathed. On the outside. Chief Russo talks briefly to the doctor and nurses, checking to see if there is anything else he can do for them. The hospital's only ambulance drives onto the playground and loads the principal and the one surviving student into the back, then pulls away slowly with its lights flashing. It will return shortly for the others, but nothing can be done for them now.

Burelle locates Hogan, but she hesitates to approach. Random lifts his head and looks around, searching for her. When he sees her, he asks Hogan to get her. The person standing over them hears the request and goes to Burelle. As Burelle walks past the covered bodies of Tom Renfroe and Grace Esch, she pauses to touch each one. She knows. Random stands and hugs his mother. Hogan wraps his arms around her and guides them into the school where it's warm. No words are spoken. In every classroom, students huddle and await the all-clear signal, wait with their teachers until a policeman will come and tell them to put their coats on and go home.

§

Inside the school Hogan guides Burelle and Random through an unmarked door to a stairwell that leads to the boiler room, a private place where only an hour earlier, Hogan shared a moment with Tom. Tom's coffee cup still sits on the custodian's wooden work desk. Hogan nudges them to a remote spot behind the boiler and sits them on a cot. On this cold December morning, the boiler hums like a locomotive. Hogan kneels in front of the devastated pair, placing a hand on each of their shoulders. He says nothing.

Random's body is calm, his eyes alert and curious about his surroundings, but he doesn't ask about the boiler room. He knows who kneels before him; he blinks and then turns his head to look at his mother. He breathes in heavily before extending his hand to take hold of hers. He feels a slight squeeze, but she doesn't turn to look at him. Random continues to look at his mother, trying to anticipate when she will break out of her trance and hug him. He waits; he's done this before, and she always responds.

Burelle sits motionless, like a statue in a cemetery. Squeezing Random's hand was an involuntary response; she doesn't know who sits beside her or who kneels in front of her. After twenty minutes her breathing slows and Hogan feels the pulse in her neck returning to normal, but still Burelle doesn't move.

Hogan pulls his hands back gently, stands, and walks away. Neither Burelle nor Random seems to care. Hogan returns quickly with a cup of water and a wet rag. He hands the water to Random and ever so gently places the rag on Burelle's neck. Random hands the cup back to his grandfather and retakes his mother's hand. Hogan lifts the cup to Burelle's lips and tilts it. Burelle opens her mouth just enough to sip. As Hogan pulls the cup back, she reaches up and takes his hands, bringing the water back to her lips. She swallows, then breathes out through her mouth.

"I can't do this anymore." She takes another drink and then pushes the cup and Hogan's hands away. She reaches around Random and pulls him close. He has not taken his eyes off of her. "I will not do this any longer." Hogan waits. "This is insane." Her jaw tightens and tears suddenly flood from her eyes. At the same moment, her lips curl as if every violent act she has suffered in her twenty-five years is coalescing in her soul. As if. Suddenly, she wails and rocks forward into Hogan's body. Burelle's sobs, her cries, are drowned out to the world by the drone of the boiler. Only Random and Hogan hear her. The two men in her life hold that life as tightly as they can, trying to save her at this moment, trying to carry her into the next moment. She shakes uncontrollably, like a naked woman cast into icy waters.

§

Hogan knows the underground tunnels of Whitman Elementary School. Around noon he carries Random and guides Burelle to an exit on the far side of the building, to the basement door away from the shooting scene. They leave the area unnoticed and walk home.

CHAPTER 31

All of Eagle Canyon is stunned. A second shooting following so close to the first one, but somehow, this one seems unlike the church shooting and unconnected. And yet, no one can clearly say why. But it is. Chief Russo comes the closest. "The church shooting was visited upon us. This one, well, it unfolded." Homemade signs appear in the windows of businesses and restaurants offering condolences. The schools close a week early for the Christmas break. The massacre is a national event, but few in town want to speak with the media. After the church shooting, Russo's wife stayed out of his way, so he could investigate the crime. On Wednesday she comes to the station to check on him because she knows he could fall apart. When he finally arrives, a little after six with the sun down, she is there with dinner. She stands and hugs him without words, but with thoughts that pass between them. Oh, God, Roos, I'm sorry. I'm here. I'm here. She will understand his guilt, but she will not agree; he had gone back to the convenience store to meet with Fulton, and that if he had gotten there five minutes earlier, he could have prevented this tragedy. Along the way, there were so many red flags.

Morvid Tree is dead, shot to death the night before by Fulton. Sergeant Collins found him on the kitchen floor, stiff and with dried blood all around him.

The wounded will survive. Don Springston and Noah Samuels. Russo takes his wife's hand and leads her to the back of his office where they sit on a bench together. "We need to go see Esch's parents again, check in on her girls. I can't do it alone, hon. You're going to need to hold me up." It was the first place Russo went after he left the school. Esch's parents already knew, but he had to see them. He held Esch's little girls, more for himself than for them. Esch's father thanked the chief, told him they would be all right, told him to go back to work where he was needed. Russo didn't want to leave. For some reason he believed he was truly needed with Esch's daughters, but he did leave. Mrs. Russo releases his hand and takes his face into both hands. "Whatever you need" is what is conveyed. Russo breaks down, leans forward onto his wife's shoulder, and surrenders. He won't cry after this night, but he needs to let go tonight, at this moment, and he cries for several minutes, his big body heaving. Finally, he regains his composure and wipes his face. "That poor woman."

"Who, dear?"

"Burelle Oakley. Her boyfriend, her best friend, the father of her child, the boy's great-grandfather." He pauses. "And Hogan. He's been trying to get some help for his son, and everybody refused. We've talked, but . . ." Russo reverts to his guilt. Even him.

After a moment Mrs. Russo, herself a big woman, takes out a tissue and wipes Russo's tears. "I can't imagine. Will the boy be okay?"

"I don't know. He's had the barrel of a gun aimed at his face twice now. Today, his father pulled the trigger and missed from ten feet away. I'd say the Lord was watching out for him, but I'm not sure the Lord was even there." Russo sees that last instant; he sees Hogan's desperate move, Fulton's distracted movement, Random Tree's defiance. Russo can still feel the recoil of his own rifle in his shoulder.

"The Lord sent you, Roos. He sent you."

§

Hogan's cigarette burns to the filter without him taking a single drag. He can't take his eyes off Burelle. She lies next to Random in Random's bed, and Hogan sits on a bare wooden chair he slid in from his bedroom. He is angry at himself for not getting Burelle and Randy out of town earlier, angry at not moving them into his house when Fulton returned from Vietnam, angry that he didn't prevent this. He will call the airlines tomorrow for reservations. He will call the West Denver Institute and tell them they are complicit. He will tell them to fuck off. He will write a letter to Tom Renfroe's parents and tell them what a fine man Tom was, and how much he respected Tom as a teacher, and that Tom was the hero at the school, that their son's actions saved many children. Hogan will drive Burelle and Randy over to Esch's parents' house to pay their respects. He will visit Don Springston in the hospital and talk. And Noah Samuels. He will keep Burelle and Randy so close that no one can get to them. No reporters this time. There is no one for them except him. And on a day in the near future, before they fly to New Zealand, Hogan will perform an act of redemption.

Burelle lies next to her son, but she remains awake. She has no words for Random or Hogan. Words have been blown out of her. One thought comes and then vanishes. Another. And another. She hears Tinker's pants. She smells the cigarette. She has another thought. She is angry at herself for not being able to concentrate. Tom. Escher. Her purse. The boiler's hum stays in her brain.

§

Arlene Dunn stands at Hogan Tree's front door. She knocks softly rather than ring the bell, feeling the latter to be intrusive. She drove over after the shootings yesterday but didn't get out of her car. She just sat and watched. Even though two children died in the shooting, Arlene feels compelled to be near the boy who survived, near the boy who was with her Billy when he was murdered, near the boy who again was targeted by a gun. This morning, twenty-six hours after the killings, she waits patiently for movement within. She will introduce herself and hopefully be asked in. She wants to sit with Burelle Oakley and her son. Somehow she knows what her purpose is: she is a lifeline.

Looking out from behind the muslin curtain hanging over the door's small window, Hogan Tree recognizes Mrs. Dunn, but he can't imagine why she would be at his door. He remembers her from the funeral, her defiance, as if she still held the essence of her son even as Billy's body lay in the coffin. She didn't cry when Billy's brother read the eulogy. Somehow, she stood apart. Hogan turns back to Burelle and Randy, nods that he will admit this person, and then opens the door.

"Hello, Mrs. Dunn. What can I do for you?" asks Hogan cautiously.

Arlene Dunn leans forward slightly, as if she's emerging from the cocoon of her heavy parka and woolen scarf that protects her from the biting cold. "I'd like to come in and sit with you all for a while. I know from my own experience how difficult these first days are, how trying the silence within the family can become. You three don't know what to say to one another, so you tend to say nothing." She pauses to let Hogan open the screen door. He does, and she steps in. Hogan takes her coat and hangs it on the hook by the door.

"Thank you, Mr. Tree." Burelle and Random stand framed in the hallway, Random just in front of his mother. Arlene gently smiles. "Hello." Her greeting is meant for both of them. She walks to them, bends and shakes Random's hand first. "Hi, Randy. My daughter Tara is in your class. She told me to tell you hi and wanted you to have this." Mrs. Dunn reaches into her pocket, takes out a baseball, and hands it to Random. "It was Billy's, but Tara wanted you to have it. We have lots of them around the house."

Random grips the ball with two fingers and his thumb on his right hand and holds it up to show Hogan. "Thank you," he says.

"You're welcome, Randy. My husband told me to tell you that he wants to be your baseball coach again next summer, so make sure you and your grandfather practice." For a moment there is silence. Then, Arlene puts her hand on Random's head and gives it a little shake. She stands to face Burelle. "May I give you a hug?"

Hogan waves to Random to come to him, and he picks up his grandson and watches. Arlene steps into Burelle and wraps her arms around the younger woman's shoulders. Arlene feels Burelle wilt slightly as if her knees were told to relax. "Let's sit down, Burelle."

Burelle and Arlene sit on the couch, and Arlene asks a tough question. "Would you tell me about Tom?" She pauses. "Everyone says what a wonderful teacher he is." She takes Burelle's hands in hers as Burelle begins to respond.

"He loved his students—and he loved me."

Hogan carries Random over and they sit next to Burelle as she tells Arlene Dunn about Tom Renfroe and Grace Esch—and about herself.

CHAPTER 32

Hogan stands silently in the cold air, but the sun warms his back. He spoke with Chief Russo the night before about any legal ramifications, and when he was assured there would be none, they relaxed like old times and talked about God. The police chief is a constant searcher about his direction, but Hogan knows his own. In one gloved hand, Hogan holds an axe: in the other a container of gasoline. Burelle sits in the station wagon and watches, unsure whether to join Hogan. Her hand rests on the door handle. A large bird rises from the treetops. Hogan sees it and turns his head into the sun to watch its flight. He turns back to Burelle and points.

Hogan surveys the area, a place he knows all too well from his childhood. Visually, it is a nearly perfect place, but evil often hides in fashionable garb. He sets the gasoline can on the snowy ground and walks to the cabin door. Decades have passed since Hogan entered this door, but what lies within remains seared in his memory. He turns sideways, raises the axe, and slams it into the door. The panel next to the lock shatters with pieces of wood flying back into Hogan's body, as if it is trying to fight back. He pulls the axe out of the door and repeats the action again and again and again. Finally, he uses the butt end of the axe to knock in the splinters. He reaches his hand inside and turns the latch on the lock, and what remains of the door swings open. Still holding the axe, Hogan steps in. The cabin creeks under his feet, as if in fear; the inside air is colder than the outside temperature, and Hogan shudders. He reaches into his coat pocket for a flashlight, switches it on, and shines its beam on his hell.

Curiosity isn't what makes Burelle lift the car door handle;

determination does. Unlike Hogan, she has been here recently. Family outings. She pulls a stocking cap over her hair and steps out into the January air, confronting her monster. Today, with its shattered door, it looks weak.

Inside, Hogan searches for specific items. He takes Pap's picture from the wall and places it in the center of the one room cabin. He removes three rifles and a pistol and stacks them near the door. He kneels to look under the adults' bed and pulls a metal box from under it. He slides a long cardboard box out that contains a wooden baseball bat, a couple of baseballs and softballs, and five old mitts. The family always played ball on the weekend overnighters. He takes the first baseman's glove, blows the dust off, and inserts his hand. He wore this glove all through high school; it's comfortable. He slams his fist into the pocket twice and imagines a ball flying into it. This glove was never here when he was young; Morvid must have brought it out after Hogan went off to college or the Navy. He slides the box to the cabin's center, puts his glove and one other next to the rifles, and returns for the metal box. It's supposed to be locked, but it isn't. A latch keeps it shut. He puts this box by the door.

Burelle keeps her distance from the cabin, but she can't keep her eyes off it. The white paint needs scrapping and repainted, as does the brown trim. The chimney has several bricks dislodged, and the ash protector has come loose. The old roof shingles need replaced, and the small porch sags. Burelle didn't notice these deficiencies before today.

Hogan checks the bureau, opens the old china cabinet, sees old cans of ham and sausages on the shelves next to the wood stove, and lifts the Coleman lanterns off their hooks. Satisfied with his inspection, he tightens his gloves and picks up the axe. With his first swing, he shatters a chair. With his second he splits the dining table. A third crushes the china cabinet. With these wood splinters, he builds a pyramid in the center of the cabin over the picture of Pap. Then, Hogan exits the cabin, taking the guns, metal box, and baseball gloves.

Burelle stands next to the gasoline can waiting. "Can't those things stay?" she asks.

"Probably, but Chief Russo told me to take them out first. Do you want to do that, or do you want me to?"

"You do it."

Hogan nods. He puts the baseball mitts in the car and lays the weapons on the ground along with the metal box. He takes the gasoline into the cabin and pours a small amount on the pyramid. He pours more on the floor, some along the edges of the cabin, and more on the wood box. Outside, he splashes most of the can's remains on the sides of the cabin. He holds up the container to Burelle offering her one more opportunity to contribute.

Burelle takes a deep breath, steeling herself to take the can. She moves to Hogan who hands her the open can. "Be careful," he warns.

"Can I go in?"

Hogan nods. "Don't touch anything." He knows where she's going.

Burelle walks cautiously into the cabin with the gas container. She moves to the bed and pours out the rest of its contents over the blankets, drops the can, and walks out. Hogan notices a slight smile on her face, a smile not of happiness, but one of something else. He isn't sure what.

"Move back to the car. This will go up hard."

§

Chief Russo stands outside his cruiser on the hill a half-mile from the Tree's cabin. He watches through binoculars and waits. He alerted the fire department that it was a controlled burn, and they were not to respond unless he called. The cabin is set apart from the trees, standing alone much like Hogan did for so many years. Russo observes Hogan come out of the cabin with the guns, sees Burelle enter the cabin with the fuel, and tenses slightly when Hogan lights the crude torch. Russo thinks about his conversation with Hogan last night, about Purgatory.

§

"I may not see Heaven, Roos, but I don't think I deserve an eternity in Hell. Maybe a middle ground."

"A long time in Purgatory, huh, Hogan?"

"Maybe. God and I aren't intimate, but we have become a bit more friendly, and He's about to provide some relief for Burelle and Randy. She wants to come with me tomorrow, but I'm taking Randy over to Esch's parents in the morning. He wouldn't understand."

Russo concurs. "His little eyes have seen too much too soon."

§

Hogan ignites a torch; a modified Molotov cocktail really, glances back at Burelle, and then tosses the bomb in the front door of the cabin. The fire erupts with a whoosh, engulfing the guts of the cabin in flames that immediately sends orange-red fingers out the windows. Hogan backs up several steps, driven back by the heat. Burelle moves to his side. They stand in silence, and Hogan reaches down to take Burelle's hand. Neither feels a sense of loss as the flames grow, surrounding the cabin in a wavy, surreal scene. The cabin crackles and pops, fizzing noises occur, pieces of wood are shot out from the structure, and black smoke rises over the flames on the roof. Burelle sees into the flames, into the place where she was raped, into the place she was forced to visit by Morvid and Fulton "for Random's good." No good ever took place in that hellish cabin. Hogan sees through the flames to the other side. If the souls of any Trees reside here, they will either be destroyed or released by the fire. A small explosion sends a partially burning two-by-four toward Burelle's feet. She picks it up and walks back to the door, now filled with flames. She tosses it back into the fire. Let nothing escape; use the cabin's parts to fuel the fire in order to complete its destruction.

§

Chief Russo drives up after the cabin has caved in upon itself, but still burns intensely: yellow near the old floor line, then orange, then red. The snow crunches beneath the cruiser's tires. Hogan and Burelle turn away from the fire to see Russo arrive. The big man climbs out of his car and moves to the couple. "That's quite a bonfire you have there."

Hogan nods, "Yep. May have overdone it with the gasoline a bit."

"Maybe, but you want to be sure." Russo puts an arm around Burelle. "You okay, young lady?" Burelle turns into the police chief's shoulder and bursts into sobs. Her body heaves. Russo allows her to cry for a moment and then speaks softly, words meant not just for Burelle, but for Hogan. "Fire is a chain reaction, you know. Just as much as it destroys, it can redeem. It just takes a little longer. After a forest fire, the trees and grasses come back stronger, healthier. Hard to see it while the flames are shooting up into the sky, when that sky is blackened by the smoke, but it's beginning at that very moment." Russo gently lifts Burelle's face off his shoulder so that he can see her eyes, so she can see his. "You've had a very difficult life up to now, but you've survived. Hogan here has purchased your life back. He tells me you have a trip planned this week. Sounds like a new beginning to me."

Burelle wipes her nose on her coat sleeve and looks to Hogan who just purses his lips. Her eyes catch movement above the smoke and she points. "There's that big bird again." Both men look.

"Well I'll be damned," says Russo. "I haven't seen an eagle around here in years. Majestic bird, isn't it."

After a few more minutes of watching the fire, Hogan speaks. "I was planning on dumping those weapons in the lake, but I think I'll dispose of them and that box of ammunition over there." He looks in the direction of the outhouse. "Unless you have a better plan."

"No. They haven't been taken good care of anyway. Come on, Burelle. You grab the ammo box."

CHAPTER 33

Chief Russo sits alone at an isolated booth with his morning coffee, his back to the main room, his head down as he studies a notebook of scribbles. Five months and three weeks have passed, school let out for the summer, tourists are visiting en masse, some for the wrong reasons, and Eagle Canyon's small, mountain town atmosphere is slowly returning. The media continues to pump out human interest stories to people a thousand miles away, to try to teach the lessons of the tragedies. Very few natives talk about the shootings anymore; everything has been said and the memories are too raw for the townspeople. Russo continues to accumulate data on the two shooters and their crimes, but to what avail? He discovered a note from Robbie written to a younger boy outlining his plans for the church shooting. The younger boy told the police chief that he never read it. Roberta at The Jungle can't recall any specific threats made by Fulton, but she knew of his anger and frustration. She should have said something, she guesses. Russo's bone tired and needs a vacation, but his sense of duty pushes him forward each day. His notebook has colored labels that he attaches to various pages so he can cross-reference information. He seldom goes on patrols as he once did, and the office routine is performed by the new man, an officer with ambitions, Esch's replacement, but fulltime.

Russo takes a letter from the notebook and rereads it. It showed up two months earlier demanding to know how Russo could allow this fraud to continue. The postmark is northern Colorado, but the writer didn't sign it. He said he drove through Eagle Canyon and saw no evidence of either shooting, that it was an obvious ruse to gain sympathy for the town that might encourage tourism and help its economy. More, the letter accused Russo of helping those groups that want to take American's guns away from them. No evidence? Russo would relish the opportunity to take the man to the cemetery to see the gravestones, or introduce him to Esch's daughters, or to have him meet the families of the murdered children. No fucking evidence? Maybe he should meet with Noah Samuels whose jaw is still wired shut. Cowards like the anonymous letter writer will remain unconvinced and hold on to their ignorant beliefs, but it rankles Russo; it sticks in his craw.

A skinny waitress with a perm warms his coffee, touches his shoulder, and points to a man standing by the register who wants to speak with the chief. She guards Russo's privacy in her restaurant. Russo nods and the man walks over to the booth. Russo knows the man well; it's Bradley Arnold's father. Russo stands and they shake hands.

"Morning, Chief. Mind if I join you for a minute. I've got to be at the shop by seven-thirty."

"No, Arnie. Sit down." The waitress pours another cup of coffee and leaves. "It's nice to have the warmer weather again."

They chat warmly. Russo doesn't mind the interruption. John Arnold has been such a steady, gentle, considerate man through all of this. Russo knew him well before the church shooting, but since that first tragedy, since his son died, since the eulogy, Russo has become even closer to Arnie. After the school shooting occurred, Arnie visited the chief several times at his home bringing food and compassion. When Mrs. Russo had no pathways to her husband's suffering or obsessions, she would call Arnie for assistance, and he was never too busy.

"What brings you in this morning?" asks Russo.

"Heard a rumor, and I wanted to get to the truth. You know about rumors." Arnie smiles over his cup and takes a sip. "Heard you were thinking about retiring."

Sipping coffee is an effective delay, an acceptable pause in a conversation to allow for a proper response. Russo sips his coffee. "You must have been talking with the missus. She's afraid that if I did, I might just drive her crazy spending all my time at home."

"She might have passed that sentiment on to my wife at the grocery store or some place." Arnie leaves it there and waits.

Russo is deliberate. "Yeah. Been giving it some thought. Maybe I could hire on at your tire place. You could do all the scheduling and finances, and I'd change all those tires."

"I suppose you'd want to get paid?"

"Minimum. I'd have my pension coming too."

Arnie rolls his tongue inside his cheek. The waitress comes by with her pot and both men accept a warmup. "I suspect you'd want time for your coffee breaks if you worked for me. And an extended lunch. And time off in the fall to go hunting?"

"Sure. Nowadays, that's what the hired help gets, isn't it?"

Arnie shakes his head. "Paid vacations for non-skilled labor. Makes you wonder, doesn't it?" Both men smile. "Nope, I don't have any openings at this time. Besides, you'd be overqualified." He sips. "Roos, I'm here to talk you out of it. Retiring. You're too good a man to be sitting on your butt all day, and you'd just rot away from the inside stewing over these events. What's done is done, but our little town has new problems, and you're the man to solve them." Arnie clasps his hands together, interlocking his fingers, and leans forward. "You've held his town together, but that doesn't permit you the leisure of stepping back yet. There's more to be done."

Russo knows there's no joking here. He leans into the table, into his friend, as if they're sharing a secret. "It's just wearing me out, Arn," he whispers. "Every damn day I play it over in my head, but when I hit the sack each night, those kids, your boy, my deputy, and the teachers, they're still dead. What do I know? What have I accomplished? I just don't think I'm getting closer to the answer, but I can't accept doing nothing. I'm accountable. I used to believe that there were sacred grounds—the churches, the schools—but both were attacked."

"That's exactly why you need to keep working, my friend. You believe you could have prevented these tragedies, should have prevented them. Most of us believe they just happened, and there's nothing we can do about the next one. You don't. That notebook attests to that. If there's something, you'll find it and pass it on to other communities. Our Eagle Canyon family doesn't blame you, never has. We appreciate what you did. But we see ourselves as isolated, that the shootings were ours and ours alone. You don't. You're a wise man, Roos, and you know this scenario could be played out in other towns, and you're fighting like hell to pass on as much information as you can glean about all this to see that it doesn't. By being the top cop here, your opinions carry weight. Other law enforcement agencies listen to you. Retire and they'll ignore you." Arnie keeps his eyes up, but he stops to sip his coffee.

"This town, all small towns, I suppose, love the simple. It's one of the reasons people choose small towns, but these tragedies have infused a messiness into our world, and it has made us uncomfortable." The big cop leans forward just a little farther. "How do you do it, Arnie? How do you stay so . . . forgiving?"

"Part of it's my faith, I suppose. This was not God's plan, nor do I blame Him for not saving Bradley. Strangely, I've moved closer to God. I feel that God hurts as much as we do, that He's appalled by what happened. I know my son is in Heaven. I stay busy. I hang around you. Being angry won't bring Bradley back. Being positive allows me to carry him around pretty easily. I once was just me, but now, to everyone I know, including you, I'm the guy whose only child was murdered, and you perceive me differently. I understand because I see myself differently. I behave differently. Heather and I make love cautiously and less often. I watch sporting events quietly." Arnie smiles. "I'm no longer the raving fan you once knew. I disposed of all my guns, several thousand dollars worth. Without Brad, I won't hunt again. I don't watch TV much anymore; read my Bible instead. Now, Roos, project that to our town. Violence bruises your soul and you change. And for each person here, that change will occur. Subtle, but real. You tell me what Eagle Canyon was, and I'll tell you what it is no longer. My son was a good boy, and, this might sound silly, but I choose to think about him and not that other boy. But someone needs to think about the other boy, beside his mom, and I guess that means you."

The big cop takes a breath and lets it out with a shudder. "I think about measures we could take to secure a school or a church; put a fence around the school, lock the doors, but I don't know how effective these would be. How could we ever secure a church? Somehow, to me, it keeps coming back to identifying the crazies before they start shooting. I should have known Fulton was dangerous, and he had all those weapons. But Robbie gave us almost no warning." Russo is berating himself as much as talking with Arnie. "Do I ever get to stop thinking about Robbie and Fulton Tree?" He pauses again. "Those two are just two. We focus on shootings with multiple deaths, but more young people, more little kids, die one at a time, one by one, each day, and no one takes responsibility. That old saying about no pebble taking responsibility for the landslide, but we have to. We're a gun culture that accepts a measure of indiscriminate violence. But that violence hit our town, and it isn't acceptable. I know that some people just shouldn't be allowed to have a gun or even be around guns."

The two men sit quietly, but their thoughts are similar. "It's a shame, Roos, our collective shame, and our children pay for it."

"I tried to ignore it too. I left Chicago and came back here where it doesn't happen. Huh! See where that got me. Seventeen years of being one of those pebbles. Every day in my country, we shoot the innocents; we slaughter them and go on."

"Stop it, Roos. You, of all people, are trying. Don't beat yourself up, but don't give up either. It's in your genes, Roos. Don't retire and let this tragedy go away, at least the lessons of these terrible things. Too many of us just want it to go away. We had a balance, but the shootings disturbed that balance. I don't know what the answers are, and I suspect you don't either. Yet. But you will. You're a good man and a good policeman. A crime was committed, and you want to get to the bottom of it. Keep working. Our town's tragedies will be a wake-up call. Things will change; you'll see."

Russo leans back and clasps his hands behind his head. He yawns. "One thing I don't get, Arnie, is that so many people I talk to get in the way." Arnie looks puzzled, and Russo notices. "It's like they think the solutions to protecting our kids might prevent them from doing something they've always done. All I want to do is keep more kids safe. I'm not blaming people who never did anything wrong, but, Jesus, I wish these people would see what one unbalanced person with a gun can do." The chief lowers his hands, placing his elbows back on the table. Almost to himself he adds, "This is such a good town with good people."

A quiet table goes quieter for a moment. Then, Arnie extends his hand across the table and lays it on the chief's forearm. "Don't let them interfere, Roos. Their fears are based on God knows what. You're the cop, and it's your job to protect us even when we don't want that protection. Our little kids can't always protect themselves yet, so you need to." Arnie leaves it at that. The two men look at each other, then nod. "I've got tires to change. Let's have our wives schedule a dinner for us soon." Arnie stands. "You have a good day, Chief."

Russo shifts in his seat and removes his billfold. He realized months ago that thinking about the two shooters all the time could destroy him, so he devised a plan to prevent that. Once a day before he goes to the office, he will remember the four students who died. He takes four pictures from his wallet and places them on the table. School pictures. Bradley Arnold, Billy Dunn, Emily Gordon, and Maggie Williams with her goofy grin and rose in her hair. I may not ever be able to stop searching for answers as to why those two young men lost their senses, but I will not forget these children. Bradley Arnold, Billy Dunn, Emily Gordon, Maggie Williams. The big man returns the photos to his wallet, leaves a five-dollar bill on the table, stands, and looks for the waitress. She's coming out of the kitchen balancing two plates of pancakes. Russo walks to the register and waits.

"Why do you always leave money, Chief? You know it's free." The waitress smells of cigarette smoke, and she reminds Russo of the sarcastic actress on TV.

"Just put it in Noah's college fund like the rest. Tell him I'll see him at practice this afternoon, okay."

CHAPTER 34

Gertie walks into the kitchen, bends over to kiss her husband on the top of his head, and takes his hand with a smile. "Come see," she says. She's a farmer: substantial, tanned, wrinkled, and forthright.

Hogan puts his fork down and rises. He will do anything she asks. "What do you have?"

"Just come see."

On the porch she points. Near the front gate, Burelle and Random play catch, a sight not often seen in rugby-crazy New Zealand. The young woman drops most of the throws, but she laughs when she does and moves quickly to recover the baseball. Her arm motion on her tosses leads to a high arching trajectory or an errant grounder, but Random doesn't care. Hogan brought the baseball mitts with him from Colorado. Random and Burelle are laughing. Six months after arriving, they are laughing. They are inseparable, chums as well as mother and son. Random laughed quickly upon getting to New Zealand, but not Burelle. He's in a growth spurt; good soil, maintains Gertie. On that first morning after arriving the afternoon before, Gertie took Burelle on a tour of her land, of her acreage, and then began instructing her on her chores. "They'll be chores at first, but soon it will become life. Trust me, dearie, these tasks will infuse energy into you."

Gertie touches her head to Hogan's shoulder, and they sit on the porch swing. "Life is all about survival, my dear. It's a chance. You and I have seen the tragedy, but we can have the beautiful too. Here, now, in this place, we are making a new life for them. Burelle's wound will never truly heal. It has left a permanent scar, but today, she's laughing. Today is another step forward."

"Grampa, come play," yells Random. Hogan pats Gertie's thigh and joins the game of catch. Burelle steps to the side to watch, allowing the throws to be more accurate. She notices Gertie watching her and nods. The corners of Burelle's mouth turn upward as she does. Each woman has the same thoughts about the other. What a beautiful, remarkable woman she is. So alone for so long, and now building a new life for herself and those around her. Gertie waves to Burelle to join her on the porch swing.

Five months earlier, the older woman heard the younger woman crying in the night. Gertie went to Burelle and held her, held her like she had held Hogan so long before, held her like a mother would hold her wounded daughter, and Gertie told Burelle the story.

"Hogan was nearly dead when I first tended to him. The nurses told me just to sit with him, just wipe his brow and hold his hand, to listen to his delirium, and not allow him to die alone. He'll tell you about his hip wound, but it was the severe head wound that was the real danger. I was just a teenager, six years younger than Hogan, just a Kiwi girl helping our boys in Australia. I learned so much from those older Australian nurses. They live in a tough land, a hard land, an often lonely land, and they grow to be tough. They're survivors too, and all had lost husbands or brothers or fathers in the war. Like you, my darling, Hogan's soul was battered, and not from the war. In his delirium he told of his abuse as a child."

Gertie rocked Burelle and told her everything about those days. Burelle relaxed and accepted Gertie's embrace. "After our children died, Hogan believed he was being punished and needed to return to America to patch things up. He's that way, you know. He holds himself responsible for every part." Gertie stopped talking and hummed a lullaby for several moments. "Violence is a disease, and once infected, it's so difficult to overcome." She paused again and hummed. "But, darling, you and Hogan are proof that a person can. Your childhoods were similar, although yours lasted longer, but you've survived. I promise you that I will not allow anyone to harm you again. Or Randy. You have my word." There were more nights of crying, and Gertie was there every time, but the healing began, and today, Burelle is laughing.

§

Hogan's new river winds northeastwards off the farm before merging with other rivers that eventually meander their way into the Bay of Plenty off New Zealand's east coast, a part of something much, much larger than itself. Hogan's is a meadow creek really; not nearly the size of Twenty-Nine Mile Creek in Eagle Canyon, Colorado, but it does contain catchable trout. He has taken up fishing again, always with a fresh stone in his pocket. Burelle and Randy carry stones too. "We don't know why, we just do it." When they are done, they return the stones to the river. Burelle dips her necklace with the yellow stone in the water each time. She walks the creek with Random and Tinker while Gertie rides her horse, but does not yet fish, although Gertie swears she will get her new daughter to do so. Randy fishes. Only his mother calls him Random any longer. His classmates know him as Randy Tree, the red-headed Yank with the funny accent.

Gertie keeps their story simple, and since she is so well respected in her agricultural setting, her neighbors accept it. Her husband Hogan returned with their grandson and Burelle after their son died in a gun incident. Painful memories too raw to elaborate on. The neighbors shook their heads and never asked again. When one of his classmates asked Randy about his father, Randy told them his pop was a teacher who died.

Farming fits Burelle. She can go hours without speaking to another soul, especially when Random attends school. Gertie keeps her busy, and every farm job is being taught to her. When Gertie put her on the tractor the first time, Burelle cast a glance at Hogan, remembering his tragedy, but he just shook his head and smiled. "It's what we do here." Oil changes and tune-ups are Hogan's job, but both Burelle and Randy are being instructed on small engines and will graduate to the tractor and station wagon in time. Burelle has cooking duties three days each week too. Winter has been harsh, with some strong winds, but like farmers and ranchers the world over, the Trees look forward to spring and the new beginning.

Dear Roos,

Raining hard here after several good days of sunshine. I'm sitting on the porch watching. I heard from Don Springston that you had a bit of a setback and are spending a few days in the hospital. If you would ever get the Internet, we could communicate a bit faster. Anyway, I hope by now you're home and feeling better, and that the doctor didn't outlaw your coffee and occasional cigar. He also mentioned that Eagle Canyon is getting a new high school. That's good news, but way overdue.

I know you've been following the events in Australia concerning gun laws. The actions of Prime Minister Howard over there have been quite courageous, but there has been strong resistance in many rural areas. Sadly, I don't see America following suit, even after some of the horrific events of the past few years. You can never hope to replicate Australia's response for so many reasons, but I wish America would earnestly try to make it more difficult—if not impossible—for its mentally disturbed young men to possess or have access to such weapons.

On the home front, Gertie keeps going, as does my love for that remarkable woman. She's in the barn as I write this brushing her horse. Randy moved to the secondary school after several years teaching in the intermediate grades. He still has an occasional dark day. Burelle's two youngest have entered university, but their hearts will bring them back to the farm. She and her husband run the place these days.

As for me, I no longer stand in the river when I fish. I cast my line from the bank these days. These days; my end of days. My river is nearing the ocean, and that is my time, as I used to tell Randy when he was a boy. I used to believe there was no such thing as time, but on windy days I can feel it rush past my cheeks. Soon, I will learn about the Great Mystery, and about the Darkness. Gertie says we have experienced that time, and now we get to enjoy our remaining days in the sunshine, this afternoon notwithstanding. Still, I wonder about that Darkness, about where it came from.

My past and present are now conjoined. My current life has merged with my past, and all that I lived is one. I have lived within those layers of darkness and survived. I am ready to meet my Maker and let him ask me that question that you once posed to me: Did I try?

Thank you for protecting my family in those dark days two decades ago, Roos—and for being my friend. Get well soon.

HOGAN

THE END